Save Us a Seat

FLETCHER McHALE

ISBN: 978-1-4834-0087-7 (sc)
ISBN: 978-1-4834-0089-1 (hc)
ISBN: 978-1-4834-0088-4 (e)

Library of Congress Control Number: 2013913037

Because of the dynamic nature of the Internet, any web addresses or links contained in
this book may have changed since publication and may no longer be valid. The views
expressed in this work are solely those of the author and do not necessarily reflect the
views of the publisher, and the publisher hereby disclaims any responsibility for them.

Certain stock imagery © Thinkstock.
Any people depicted in stock imagery provided by Thinkstock are models,
and such images are being used for illustrative purposes only.

Lulu Publishing Services rev. date: 7/16/2013

For Lynno … Not a day goes by that I don't miss you

Acknowledgments

I have always been blessed with loving and supportive people, they are priceless to me.

Mama and Daddy, thank you for not killing me on the many, many occasions you probably should have. Maybe I haven't always acted like it, but I have always appreciated the way you both have pushed me to be a better person. I love you both so much.

Em, what can I say? Do you have any idea what a gift you are to me? You were there when being there wasn't a popular place. I will never forget that. When people describe what a best friend should be, surely they use you as an example.

Shell, I know who sent you … she's a sneaky girl. I didn't expect to find another BFF this late in the game, but there you were. Thank you for shoving me even when I don't want to be shoved.

Beck … my hero. You are a constant source of inspiration for me, and you don't even know it. I am so glad you love me just a little bit more than you want to choke me!

Fern Land and Tommy Ray Harrison, thank you for sharing the power of words with me. I love you Mrs. Land….I miss you, Tommy Ray.

Micki, your words gave me a ton of confidence. Whatcha gonna do with all those feathers, girl?

Lea, God sure knew what He was doing when He sent you to me. You have always been my biggest cheerleader no matter the struggle. Nothing is more precious to me than you and the other three people in your house!

JW... Did you ever think we'd find ourselves here? You have always been the unwavering calm in my crazy, crazy life. No matter what cliff I am teetering on, you are always there to pull me back. I love my Baby Daddy.

Greg, if it's keeping me well or making me laugh until my sides hurt, you have the prescription. I love you, Doc.

Melinda, there are so many things I could've never done without you. Thank you for your patience, your calm and your loyalty. I love you, friend.

Darlene, Rachel, Cindy, Keli, Laura Jean and Susie ... Thank you all so much for always believing in me, no matter what. You made me believe too.

To the rest of my family, my brother, sister-in-law, nieces, nephews, and their families, I love you all more than you could ever know. The happiest times in my life are when we're all together.

Some people go to priests; others to poetry; I to my friends.
—Virginia Woolf

Chapter 1

*T*his should have been an incredibly exciting evening for me. I'd certainly waited on it long enough. After weeks of flirting, texting, stolen glances, and closet phone calls, the object of my obsession, my secret, was here in my arms. Finally! And he was whispering words I had longed to hear. "Divorce him. I love you! Marry me." For what seemed like an all-too-brief moment, it was indeed magical, earth-shattering, heavenly-choir-inducing, and perfect. Then my conscience began banging on the door. Literally.

"Carrigan!" My conscience, aka my best friend, Laine Landry, shouted through the door. "I swear I will knock this door down if I have to!"

I knew she was serious. She had begun lightly tapping thirty minutes earlier and was now engaging in a frenzied flurry of sharp raps about every ninety seconds. But the laughter that welled up inside me and the god of a man lying beside me outweighed the threat of her foot coming through the door. Besides, she'd threatened bodily harm, poisonous gas, and police invasion before. But I'd never seen any of those things happen. Sometimes my girl was just all bark. I decided to test the waters.

"I'm not ready to leave!" I shouted at the unwanted intrusion. "Go away! Come back in an hour." I snuggled closer to my lover and pulled the covers up around my head.

"Carrigan, I am *not* playing with you!" she said, louder this time.

"Jack is gonna start looking for us! I'm not gonna get shot because you're an idiot!"

I rolled my eyes. "Jack would never shoot you!" I yelled back and then turned to my secret and said, "He may shoot *you*, but he'd never shoot *her*." I wasn't sure, but I thought I detected a slight look of concern on his face. Of course, that could have been the tequila making me imagine things. Or maybe that was just the way he always looked.

"*Now!*" Laine said, this time through gritted teeth. For some reason, that was really funny to me and to Adonis who, God bless him, probably couldn't spell Adonis but would damn sure look good trying to.

"One, two ..." Her voice was louder this time.

Hell, she was counting now. That was never a good sign. I had been on the receiving end of her infamous counting a few times before, and it had never turned out well for me. If she got to twenty, she lost her mind, and being in a corridor of a hotel at two a.m. would make no difference to her at all. Shit just got real.

"Okay!" I shouted back and began moving. "Give me a few minutes!"

"Three, four ..." she continued, each number louder than the last.

I was sure the entire wing of the Holiday Inn Express was on full alert as I frantically began searching for clothing. Where the hell were my shoes? Had I worn shoes? And hadn't there been a bra at some point? A flimsy, lacy, tiny thing that had replaced my ever-present sports bra for this most special occasion? I danced around the bed naked, digging for apparel, and slapped at Adonis's hand as he reached for me.

I know how this will sound, but I had no issue and no remorse over being in a hotel room with a man who wasn't my husband. But my best friend was having some major issues with it. I knew if she got to the number twenty, everybody that occupied a space near Room 224 was about to be informed of my ... um ... indiscretion. So I was in a hell of a hurry. I finally found the bra on the lamp shade and stuffed it in my purse. I pulled on a version of the outfit I had showed up in, kissed Adonis, promising to call him tomorrow, and grabbed my shoes on the way out the door.

Laine was pacing the hallway, red-faced and about to scream, "Twenty!" when I gently closed the door behind me. I smiled broadly, trying to soften the irritation on her face, but I am pretty sure she could have punched me right then.

"Oh, you think this is funny?" she demanded, her hands on her hips. "What the hell is wrong with you? Do you know what time it is? You know Jack is looking for us! What if he sees the car? What if he's outside waiting for us? What the hell is wrong with you?" She gestured wildly.

I could see right away any conversation I started would head south pretty quickly, so I decided to let her continue ranting for another minute or two. I thought maybe it would squelch her paranoia. But that proved to be futile. She didn't lower her voice either. In fact, the more she talked, the shriller her voice became. I was sure it was now at a decibel reserved for the training of golden retrievers. In fact, I expected a pack of dogs to turn the corner any second. My only goal at this point was to get her out of this hallway before security came around.

I was dragging her by the arm when the hairiest man I have ever seen stuck his disrobed upper torso out of his room. "What the hell is going on out here?" he demanded.

"Oh shit!" I said, his werewolf body startling me. The dogs *had* heard her! "LSD flashback." I flashed him a smile and continued pulling Laine toward the exit. Thankfully, Sasquatch mumbled something I couldn't understand and then went back into his cave.

Laine stopped in her tracks and stared at me. "You lie so easily now it frightens me," she said, throwing her arms in the air. "Who *are* you?"

I laughed at her expression and kept nudging her toward the exit. I couldn't think about that accusation too much. Mostly because she had spoken the truth. Lying had become too frequent and too easy for me. I lied all the time—to my parents, to my in-laws, and especially to my husband. But I was having an affair, dammit! What was I supposed to do? Affairs didn't happen in church. They happened at the Holiday Inn Express in Shreveport. And you *lied* about it. I could just see the chaos telling the truth would cause. Besides, they would all find out soon enough, just as soon as I got up enough courage to ask for a divorce. That thought made me frown. I pushed the twinge of guilt from my mind and trudged forward. Damn, it was hard to walk fast in what Laine described as "hooker heels." No wonder all the prostitutes on television were pissed off all the time.

I decided to try a new approach. Twenty-plus years experience with my soul sister, conscience, and best friend had taught me that making her laugh was the quickest way to diffuse a situation. Only I was still intoxicated, figuratively and literally by the touch of the man I'd made love to and the half bottle of tequila I had ingested before doing so. My wits weren't as sharp as usual, so I said the only thing I could think of. "How was the movie?"

Laine stopped again, looked at the floor, tapped her foot, and shook her head. "Really?" she asked, her voice dripping with disgust.

Her stance made me laugh instead. "Come on, Laine," I said. "It's okay! Jack isn't looking for us, I promise. I would bet my best boots that he is leaning up against a bar somewhere trying to coax a phone number out of a chick with big boobs and blond hair. We are the last things on his mind. Especially me. Trust me on that one."

That had seemed to momentarily calm her somewhat. At least she had stopped screeching. But when we got to the parking lot, she was on high alert again, slinking around corners and moving like a cat. If she'd pulled out a finger gun, I wouldn't have been surprised.

I sighed, watching her. "Give me my keys," I said as we approached my black Camaro. I tried to snatch them from her hand.

"Are you crazy?" she asked for the forty-second time in five minutes. "I can smell the alcohol from over here! You aren't killing me tonight."

I shook my head. "Drama queen," I muttered.

"Tequila breath," she retorted.

I knew I was fighting a losing battle and stood by the passenger door, waiting for her to pop the lock. I hated for somebody else to drive my car. Even Laine. I loved this car. For some reason, I felt invincible in it and much like a goddess. That was probably some undiagnosed Freudian thing, but I didn't care. I felt untouchable in it, although I had no idea why. I stayed in some sort of minidrama all the time. It was really quite exhausting.

"Well?" Laine said as we left the parking lot, finally secure in the facts that we had escaped and that Jack wasn't lurking around with a tire iron.

I had assured her for months that Jack didn't care enough to come looking for me, regardless of where I went or how long I stayed away. She always answered with the same sentence. "He loves you more than either of you know." I had no idea why she believed that, and when I pressed her, she never had an explanation. She just insisted that it was true. But I didn't believe it for a second. If Jack was still in love with me, he certainly had an odd way of showing it.

"Well, what?" I answered, even though I knew what she wanted to know. What had transpired between Adonis and me? Had tonight been all I had hoped for?

"What happened?" she demanded and then put her hand up. "And please, spare me the play by play. I just want the verbal exchange. Nothing else!"

I laughed, leaned my head back against the seat, and closed my eyes. The tequila and the rush of being with him were catching up with me. I was suddenly very tired. "It was good, it really was." I braced myself for the reaction I knew I would get with the next sentence. "He wants me to divorce Jack and marry him." I bit my lip. Something about saying that out loud bothered me. And I didn't like it.

"Surely you aren't considering that?" she asked in a panicked voice, and before I could answer, she added, "And just so you know, I think it would be a terrible mistake."

"Well, Laine, I had no doubt you would," I answered, irritated now with her quick response. Her unwanted opinion exasperated me, and I didn't care to discuss it with her anymore. "I'm gonna close my eyes for a little while. Just get us home. We'll talk about it tomorrow."

I had expected an argument but she'd surprisingly let it go, turned the radio up, and drove in silence. I was certainly glad she did.

I didn't understand Laine sometimes. She adored Jack even though she knew he'd been unfaithful to me. Before I had ever entertained the thought of cheating on him, he had cheated on me. At least I was relatively sure that he had. But Laine always seemed to take up for him, always insisting that he loved me and encouraging me to hang on, to try one more time. It irritated the hell out of me. She was *my* best friend. She and Ella Rae Weeks were the anchors in my oh-so-rocky life. Ella Rae had never encouraged me to stay with Jack. She didn't care where I was as long as I was happy. Why did Laine constantly insist that I stay? A better question, *How* could Laine insist that I stay? She'd seen me fret and worry over Jack for two years. Of course, those emotions had eventually turned into defiance, which led us to where we were tonight. But they had still driven me crazy, and she had watched. Yet any time we had words about it, she would never back down. "He loves you, and you love him" was her standard answer for every situation I found myself in with Jack. Only it wasn't an answer; more like a declarative statement. Period. The end. No explanations needed.

I sighed. It frustrated me, made me mad, but more than anything else, hurt my feelings. I felt that Laine was choosing Jack over me. Still, I consoled myself in the fact that she just really had no idea what a relationship was like. She'd never been in one. Not a long term one, at least. I would never be able to convince her how twisted and complicated things can get years into a marriage, even if you still really did love each other. Sometimes loving each other wasn't enough. And I wasn't sure that Jack and I even had that left. We seemed more like strangers who shared a residence.

That thought made me sad, and I didn't want to be sad tonight, so I shoved it from my mind and conjured up the image of the man I had just left, wanting more. He was truly one of God's finest specimens. Not the sharpest tool in the shed, but I hadn't really been interested in talking. I smiled at the memory. If I was lucky, maybe I would dream about him too.

"Wake up, Carrigan!" The voice seemed terribly far away. "We're home! *Get up!* Jack is here!"

Ugh ... sleep drool. I wiped at it and opened my eyes. "Calm down, Laine," I said. "He does live here. Besides, he's as guilty as I am." I rubbed my eyes, trying to wake up. The tequila didn't feel so smooth on my stomach now.

"Are you ill?" she asked, a little too sarcastically.

"I'm fine," I lied. "Go home. I'll see you in the morning."

"It is 'in the morning,'" she corrected.

"You know what I mean!"

"Okay, but you have *got* to stop this, Carrigan."

I shook my head. Here we go.

"You have to grow up sometime," she continued. "You can't just go around doing this forever. You know?"

No point in arguing. "I know you're right," I said. Of course I didn't mean it, but it was an effort to make her shut up. "Get your ass across the street while I watch you. I can't go to bed wondering if a serial killer got you." I propped against the car and watched as she walked into the dark, still talking over her shoulder.

"Okay, but I'm not kidding. You're too old for this, and I am too. It's three a.m. I have to be at the ballpark in about four hours, Carri. This is ridiculous."

Laine was saying some more stuff too, but I'd turned her off after the "this is ridiculous" remark. I watched as she flipped on her porch light and entered the side door to her kitchen. I looked at my own door then and sighed. I dreaded going inside. You shouldn't have to feel this way in your own home. Home should be a place you looked forward to. But I avoided mine like the plague. Maybe Jack wouldn't speak to me when I walked in. I just didn't have it in me to fight tonight.

I toyed with the idea of sleeping in the car; after all, I had slept in it before. But I was already busted anyway. I had seen Jack peering out the window when we drove up. I may as well go in and begin sparring. Fighting seemed to be our only means of communication these days. We either didn't talk at all or we bickered. But the last thing I wanted to do tonight was have a shouting match. When I was on top of my game, I could hold my own against a verbal assault from anybody. But tonight I simply did not want to fight. I was tired, still drunk, and for some reason I couldn't fathom, sad.

As soon as I put my key into the lock and stepped inside, I heard the thinly veiled accusation.

"It's three a.m., Carrigan. Where have you been?" Jack's blue eyes were steely, and I could see the controlled rage on his face.

I stuck my chin up defiantly and stared back. I might not have wanted to fight, but if he was going to pick one, I would certainly engage. "Please, Jack, don't act like you care where I've been." I dropped my purse and keys on the table beside the door and stepped out of my shoes. "I'm going to bed." I walked away.

Expecting him to follow me, I was actually surprised when I heard the front door close. Then I heard his truck start as I stripped off my clothes and fell into bed. *Good*, I thought to myself. *One less thing to deal with tonight.* I was asleep as soon as my head hit the pillow.

Chapter 2

*E*lla Rae showed up at the crack of dawn. Actually, it was the crack of noon; it just *felt* like dawn. But the virtual love hangover and the quite real tequila hangover made it feel like five a.m. As usual, Ella Rae didn't care what kind of shape a person was in, and she dove into the bed with me.

"Get up!" she shouted. "We play in exactly forty-five minutes."

She had scared the hell out of me when she jumped into the bed, and my heart was still pounding. "Ugh," I moaned and turned over, wrapping my head up in my pillow. "I can't play softball today. I'll die. I'm not going."

She ripped the covers from me. "Oh yes you *are* going," she said. "And put some clothes on. Nobody wants to see your naked ass."

I tugged at the covers, "You've seen me naked maybe a thousand times," I said. "I can't play today. I just can't."

"Seeing your cookie when you get in and out of the tanning bed isn't the same thing," she said. "And nobody dies from a hangover. Go puke if you need to, but hurry up!"

I lay motionless. "Two more minutes," I begged.

Ella Rae sighed. "Fine. Tell me about the big stud last night. And please … be as graphic as you like!"

I sat up then, alarmed. "Where's Jack?"

She looked at me like I was insane. "He left as soon as he let me in. Do you think I'm crazy? Asking about last night with Jack in the next room?" She reached into the suitcase she called a purse, pulled out an ancient Rubik's cube, and began twisting it. "This thing annoys me," she said.

I shook my head. Ella Rae's attention span was three to five seconds long. Shorter if alcohol was involved.

"Thank God Jack is gone," I said. "I thought maybe you'd switched over to Laine's team." I looked around. "Where *is* Laine?"

"She had to be there at eight this morning, remember? She's keeping score."

"Oh yeah," I said. "I think she mentioned that as she was shrieking outside my hotel room door last night." I cringed at the memory of Sasquatch and his hairy chest. I wondered if he'd taken a silver bullet during the night.

"What?" Ella Rae threw the Rubik's cube back into her purse. "Do tell!"

I rolled my eyes. "She *counted!*" I said.

"Oh crap!" Ella Rae had been on the receiving end of Laine's counting a few times herself. But her only sins involved alcohol and a very loud and very smart mouth.

"Typical Laine," I said. "You know, the usual, 'Jack is gonna kill us, he's gonna be in the parking lot, he's waiting with a gun.' The same song and dance. I love her, God knows I do. But she's so … responsible."

Ella Rae laughed. "One of us has to be." She walked to my dresser and began fishing for clothes. "Get in the shower and hurry. I'll find you something to put on."

I stood up and groaned. I could feel the remains of last night all over my body. "I'll be ten minutes." I moved gingerly toward the bathroom. I stood in the shower, letting the hot water pour directly onto my face for ten minutes. It felt like heaven.

"Hurry up!" Ella Rae slapped the shower curtain.

"I am hurrying!"

"Bullshit," she called. "You're standing in one spot, trying to recover. I know you. Now hurry up!"

"Fine," I said and grabbed the shampoo bottle.

The softball tournament we were playing in was a benefit for a five-year-old child in our community who had recently been diagnosed with leukemia. His name was Dakota. Sweetest little guy in the world. Ella Rae, Laine, and I had gone to high school with his parents. Good people. Laine had helped put this tournament together. Thankfully, Dakota's prognosis was excellent, but the frequent trip to Saint Jude's Children's Hospital in Memphis was taking a financial toll on his family, so all the proceeds of the tournament would go directly to his family to help with those expenses.

That was one of the perks of living in a small, southern town. Among other things, we came to each other's aid. Bon Dieu Falls, Louisiana, was no different. When one of our own was in trouble, we showed up. We baked, we baby sat, and we gave cars, time, and money. Nobody could ever accuse us of being unfeeling or uncaring.

But the flip side of that coin remained as well. Your personal business was also everybody else's. The old adage "When I don't know what I'm doing, somebody else always does" fit my town like a glove. For a girl like me, that was sometimes quite annoying. Not that I was a wild child. Hell, I was no child at all. But I was, well, busy. That's a good word, and one my parents would no doubt endorse. I was twenty-eight years old, but every time someone asked my age, my immediate thought was seventeen. I often wondered how long that number would stick in my brain and why it was stuck there in the first place. Maybe it was because I had married Jack when I was seventeen. Maybe I felt permanently trapped there, like I was holding my breath, waiting for my life to begin again. Maybe the years in between were just really long seconds and one day I would inhale again and turn eighteen.

Jack Whitfield III was ten years my senior. His family owned and operated Whitfield Farms, a hugely successful soybean farm and cattle ranch. He was extremely handsome, and his seemingly cool and detached attitude made him all the more attractive. He was considered the catch of the town for years, but no one could seem to make him commit or tie him down for long.

I always felt the reason I had succeeded was that I wasn't trying. At least not in the beginning. I had just wanted to have some fun and maybe irritate my parents a little, as I was a bit rebellious in my teenage years. Okay, I was a *lot* rebellious in my teenage years. I just liked to test my limits, no matter what I was doing. So I did. With grades, ignoring curfews, ignoring expectations. I felt … different. That's about as well as I can explain it. I felt that the rules didn't really apply to me. Not in an "I am better than you" kind of way; more like "that rule is stupid" kind of way. I had a hard time relating to people who just accepted all their restrictions without question. Besides, I had always been able to talk my way out of any situation I found myself in. That in itself made me feel out of step with the rest of the world around me. While everyone else seemed to struggle to find their voice, words flew out of my mouth at the speed of light. That wasn't always a good thing, but it was pretty much always an effective thing one way or the other. I never understood what was so difficult about just saying whatever was on your mind. But sometimes folks looked at me like I was an alien. Regardless, I'm not sure my parents found the trait quite as endearing as Jack Whitfield III had found it. He told me once it was what had made me irresistible to him.

My parents were less than pleased when I announced I was dating a man ten years my senior whose womanizing reputation preceded him. But I think they knew me well enough to know fighting it was pointless. They were always cordial when he came to the house to see me or to pick me up. But they didn't like it, not one little bit. They reminded me often of the age difference and the problems that went along with that—whatever that was supposed to mean.

Then one night, Daddy told me Jack Whitfield III "had a way with women," and I replied, "I certainly hope so." My father was less than impressed with that answer, and an argument ensued. Daddy ended the argument by saying he forbade me to see Jack again. He may as well have told me not to breathe.

I failed to mention the argument to Jack. Looking back, I am sure he would've done the honorable thing and backed off. But I wasn't about to let somebody else tell me how to live my life. Not even my parents. As much as I loved them, this was *my* life. So for the next couple of weeks, I got pretty slick about hiding my relationship with Jack from them until they backed off a little bit.

On the Friday exactly two weeks after I had gotten the "I forbid you to see him" speech from Daddy, Jack and I picked up Ella Rae and Laine, drove to Texas, found a justice of the peace, and got married. I had managed to con Jack into believing that my parents, while not happy about it, had consented to the elopement. He questioned me, of course, but I told him they understood what we were doing but didn't want to be a part of it. I had even produced the proper legal document showing my father's signature allowing me to do so. It was forged, of course, but Jack didn't know that. He had wanted to talk to my father face-to-face, but I had convinced him it was unnecessary and would probably be unwelcomed. "Let's just go," I had said. "Don't make it any harder than it has to be. He'll just try to talk us out of it. Don't you want to marry me?" It had taken quite a performance, one that surely warranted an academy award.

Ella Rae had been on board immediately. It took a little coaxing for Laine. She had been mortified at the prospect of deceiving Jack and my parents. Hell, Laine felt bad if she gave the dog the cheap biscuits. She apologized to Jack for *years* afterward. But he always smiled and told her the same thing. "Laine, she could sell ice to the Eskimos. Let it go."

After the three-minute wedding ceremony and a honeymoon the next day at a huge Texas water park, Ella Rae and I felt grown up, superior, extremely adventurous, and quite pleased with ourselves, but Laine bit her fingernails and wrung her hands for three days. And I have to admit, her paranoia was right on the money. When we got home, there was a big ole small-town mess waiting on all of us. My parents were infuriated and threatened to have Jack arrested. Jack was infuriated with me for lying to him, and his parents were mortified. Laine's mother threatened to break her arm off and beat her with it, and Ella Rae's mother glared at her for thirty straight minutes before she ever said a word.

In the end, my parents knew they were fighting a losing battle and relented. But they insisted that we have a small and proper wedding the next weekend in our church. Jack was pretty unhappy with me for a few days. In fact, I wasn't entirely sure he'd show up at church the next Friday night, but he did. And he sure looked good standing at the end of the aisle waiting for me with a huge smile on his face.

We settled into our new home on my eighteenth birthday, and life was beautiful. We were young and happy and in control of our lives. Our house was the hangout in town for all our friends, and they were there nearly twenty-four hours a day. Jack adored me, couldn't get enough of me, and catered to my every whim. He said I made him laugh—in the beginning.

"Let's go, Carrigan!" Ella Rae's voice was urgent now. "We play in thirty minutes!"

Dear Lord, how was I going to stand in the boiling sun today? "I'm ready!" I shouted through the bathroom door.

"Get your bat and glove," she reminded me.

"Already in the car," I said. "I anticipated my condition this morning, so I loaded all my stuff before my little trip last night."

Ella Rae beamed at me like I'd won the Nobel Prize for Good Thinking. "Good call!"

I chuckled. Ella Rae woke up in a new world every morning.

The ballpark was a three-minute drive from my house. Ella Rae and I usually jogged there and back every morning while Laine rode circles around us on her bike, a ritual we had practiced for years, rain or shine, hot or cold, hungover or sober. We had also played softball at this park since we were five years old. Laine had kept the scorebook since she was old enough to figure it out. She wasn't "athletically inclined" as she liked to put it. Ella Rae and I called it "lazy," but Laine didn't care what we called it. She wasn't about to give up her comfortable chair, the huge purple-and-gold beach umbrella she sat under, or her cutesy flip flops for cleats, dirt, and sweat on the field.

As soon as we arrived, I dragged my chair under Laine's umbrella and hid from the sun.

"And how do we feel this morning?" Laine asked a little too sweetly.

I closed my eyes behind my dark sunglasses. "I know you're going to enjoy this," I said. "Go ahead, jab me."

"Oh, I'm not going to jab you," she assured. "You slept a total of eight hours, and I slept a total of three. I'm too exhausted to jab you."

Ah, she was going the guilt-trip route. Classic Laine. She was a travel agent for guilt trips. "I owe you one," I said.

"You owe me about 120, but who's counting?" she said, again too sweetly. But finally, she broke a smile. "It's fine, really." She lowered her voice. "Were you in trouble with Jack?"

I shrugged. "He asked where I'd been and then left. I'm sure he had somewhere of his own to go."

"Whatever you say."

I rolled my eyes and put my glove over my face. There was no way I was getting into an argument with Laine this morning. I barely had enough stamina to sit upright in the chair. If she wanted to spar, she was going to have to do it by herself. And what was that stench coming from the canteen? Cotton candy? Pure hot, sticky sugar? Tequila had historically given me liquid courage at night and horrendous nausea the next day. I fought the urge to gag and took a sip of my bottled water.

"Hey, Miss Landry!" I heard a small child say.

"Hey, King!" Laine answered.

Oh crap. That badass Thompson kid. Who the hell names their child "King" anyway? He was stirring greasy nachos with his grubby little fingers. I had to look away.

"Whatcha doin'?" He flung half his cheese mixture onto the quilt we sat on under the umbrella.

Ugh! My gag reflex went from zero to sixty. Those grimy fingers and that greasy cheese coupled with the cotton candy smell from the canteen was about to make me projectile vomit.

"I'm just keeping score," Laine told him. "What are you doing?"

"I'm just watching my daddy play ball," he said, grinning as he swiped at the cheese on his chin.

"Okay, Prince, Deuce, Ace, whatever your name is. Shoo! Run away!" I scooted back in my chair.

"Bye!" He shouted and ran off.

"Carrigan!" Laine scolded. "That was so rude! He is a child!"

"Yes. A child that was close to getting puked on."

"Hey, y'all!" another too-sweet drawl greeted. I looked up into the sun and nearly died on the spot from the brightness. Bethany Wilkes stood in front of me, and another wave of nausea washed over me. If this didn't finish me off, nothing would. Her hair was too blond, her lips were too red, her fingernails were too long, and her boobs were too fake. Missile tits, as my girls and I referred to them. How did you even get your boobies to point like that? Were there special bras for that? Was that actually Victoria's secret? Also, I had never once seen her wear a pair of shoes that I liked, and today was no exception. Were those feathers? I rolled my eyes behind my sunglasses.

Bethany wanted Jack so badly she could taste it, and everybody in Bon Dieu Falls knew it, including me. *Especially* me. I wasn't entirely sure she hadn't already had him. The curiosity was killing me, but for now, all I had was speculation, no proof. If I accused her, it would make me seem weak and insecure. If I accused him, it would seem like I cared. So I watched and waited all the time for my "gotcha" moment. Until then, I had to force myself to be cordial. I almost gagged at the concept among other things. I kicked at the nacho cheese on the quilt and smiled broadly at Bethany.

"Hi, Bethany," I said in my friendliest voice. "How's it going?"

"It's just going great!" she gushed. "How are you ladies?"

"It's all good." I smiled.

I could feel Laine trying not to laugh, which was her reaction to anything uncomfortable. And I was glad Ella Rae was already in the dugout because she would have glared and made that snarly thing with her lip, which was *her* reaction to anything uncomfortable.

"How's your new job?" Laine asked, and I could've kicked her. Dammit, now we're having a conversation.

"Oh, it's the best job!" Bethany nearly shouted. "I just don't know how they survived until I got there! Those books were a mess!"

Sweet Jesus! She worked part-time at a small bakery in the next town. They couldn't have sold more than ten cupcakes a day. How bad could the books be? Was somebody missing a quarter? But on the other hand, I sincerely hoped she would eat her way through the summer. She was much thinner than I was, and I only weighed 120 pounds. Did this chick eat at all? Probably all the time. Another reason to be annoyed with her. I wanted to drag her out to the parking lot and beat the hell out of her, but she'd probably even bleed cute.

"They are lucky to have you, Bethany," I lied, and Laine coughed. "Well, looks like it's just about game time. It was good to see you." I lied again and tried to pull my tired body and aching head out of my chair gracefully.

"Carrigan." Bethany grazed my arm with her red claws. "Where is your good-looking husband? I need to talk a little business with him."

About what? Chocolate icing? "I don't know where he got off to," I said sweetly while I seethed inside. I looked around, and I'll be damned if the son of a bitch wasn't driving up. "Today's your lucky day, girl." I pointed toward the parking lot.

She fluttered off all white and poofy and lacy with her ugly sandals to talk "business" with my husband. Who the hell wears all white to the ballpark?

"Bye, now!" she called to us over her shoulder.

I looked down at my t-shirt, cutoff jeans, and cleats, feeling a little bit like a dirt farmer who had just spoken to a supermodel. This was certainly shaping up to be a stellar day.

"Bye, now," Laine mocked as I gathered my glove and bat and headed to the dugout.

"Oh, kiss my ass," I said and heard her laughter behind me.

Mercifully, we lost the game. There were so many entries in this tournament; it was single elimination, so we were done for the day. As competitive as I am, I would have never tried to lose on purpose, but I certainly wasn't upset that we lost. I had spent most of the game in left field trying to see what Jack and Bethany were doing without looking like I was trying to see what they were doing. I told myself I was only making sure Jack wasn't making a spectacle of himself by allowing Bethany to hang all over him. In reality, I was trying to stifle the voice inside me that kept accusing me of being jealous. It's a very irritating voice, by the way. I could usually shut it up by thinking about Adonis, but it was quite a little chatterbox today.

Most of the time, Jack, Bethany, and a couple of Jack's friends were standing a few feet from our dugout, talking and laughing. Bethany must have touched Jack's arm fifty times. Couldn't she speak without using her hands? I missed a fly ball while she told an entire story with her arm on his waist. His waist! Seriously! How many people talk to somebody with their hand on their stomach? I was furious. I had to hand it to Jack, though. He looked very uncomfortable, and that made me very happy.

When the game was over, Jack, Bethany, and their little group were still talking. Ella Rae and I brought our things over to Laine's blanket and dove under the umbrella.

"Nice game," Laine said and smiled.

"Ha ha," I said. "I don't feel well." Lying down, I put my glove over my face.

"And whose fault is that?"

I sighed. "I acknowledge that I may have made a couple of poor choices last night."

"Hmpf," Laine snorted.

"You need to bitch slap Bethany Wilkes," Ella Rae announced out of nowhere in her pissed-off voice, which was very loud, almost as loud as her drunk voice.

"Shut up, Ella Rae!" I said. "And stop looking at them!" I certainly didn't want either Jack or Bethany to think I cared what they were doing or saying.

"I can't believe you're just sitting here!" she said indignantly and without lowering her voice an octave. "I can promise you, she'd be wearing that little 'screw me' shirt around her neck if she was saddled up with Tommy like that!"

"Tommy wouldn't be over there," I said, irritated. "He's a *real* husband."

"Jack is a real husband, too, Carrigan," Laine chimed in. "You need to take yourself over there, and slide *your* arm around his waist!" She turned her attention to Ella Rae. "And will you stop encouraging her to get angry?"

"Are you kidding me?" Ella Rae retorted. "She'd have to be blind not to be pissed!"

"It doesn't matter," I said. "If my hair was on fire and Jack had the only bucket of water in town, I wouldn't go over there. So just stop it. And Ella Rae, stop looking at them, dammit!"

"Good!" Ella Rae said. "You don't need to go over there. He needs to bring his ass over here."

"You're both crazy," Laine said, shaking her head. "He's *your* husband."

"My point exactly," I said. "This discussion is over. Besides, you need to pay attention to this game. You just missed a run."

Laine went back to her scorebook, but I was sure this conversation wasn't really over.

I lay back down and groaned. "I am so ready to go home," I said.

"Oh no!" Laine nearly shouted, "You aren't going anywhere! I stayed with you last night, so you're staying with me today until the bitter end."

There was no point in arguing with her, so I decided that I may as well make myself comfortable. I propped a pillow on top of my bat bag and stole a glance at my husband, Marilyn Monroe Jr., and their entourage. Yep, still there. I laid my head down and closed my eyes. *I may have to be here*, I thought. *But I don't have to communicate.*

I took a few catnaps here and there during the day, but there was really no rest for the weary. Another thing about a small town is that there is no such thing as anonymity. Everybody knows everybody else, and most of them feel compelled to talk to you. I find this extremely unnecessary. Small talk annoyed me; call me when something important happens and we can avoid all this "how's the weather" business. However, that just isn't the way it works. So our conversations that day ranged from ugly shoes, our new pastor at church, the Thompsons' choice of baby names, Sara Greer's gallbladder, and what design Otis Moore had painted on the Bon Dieu Falls water tower this month. Some said a dragonfly, others claimed a buzzard, but we all agreed on one thing: How in the world did he keep crawling up that water tower without getting caught or killed?

Otis had been fondly referred to as the town drunk for as far back as I could remember. He slept in a shed by the depot most nights, even though he had a home and a common-law wife. One of the older Thompson kids, Mackerel I believe was his name (and no, I'm not kidding), told me "town drunk" was not a politically correct term anymore. He said Otis Moore was "beer challenged." I asked Ella Rae who that child was when he walked away, and she said, "Village Idiot." Such is life in a small town.

Ella Rae was going to have a hell of a crick in her neck the next day because she'd spent most of it looking sideways at Jack and Bethany Wilkes and giving me a play by play for the last two games. She reported Jack had tried to walk away several times, but Red Claws kept pulling him back in. What the hell? Jack was over six feet tall and two hundred pounds with arms like a steel beam. He couldn't get away from that pasty-faced piece of painted pine straw? What a guy. I wanted to punch him in the mouth. I turned over on my stomach and demanded she not tell me another thing.

A little while later, Bethany apparently loosened her grip because Jack came and sat down under the umbrella with us. Bethany stayed put with a swarm of men but laughed too loudly and stared too much at our little oasis. I had to turn and face Jack to keep myself from making ten-year-old faces at her. My inner child was aching to jump up and down, stick my tongue out, and sing, "Nanny nanny boo boo!"

I tried to fake sleep for a while. I was furious with Jack for talking to Bethany for so long and furious with myself for caring. Finally, I sat up and forced myself to be pleasant. There was one thing I knew for certain about Jack Whitfield III—he loved Ella Rae and Laine and would never do anything to disrespect either of them. That had always kept a soft spot in my heart for him. He wouldn't even argue with me in front of them. If we ever had angry words in their presence, it was because I had started them, but he shut them down.

"Where is Tommy today, Rae?" Jack asked.

"He's fishing again." She rolled her eyes. "I don't know why he's fishing again, but he is. We have so much fish in the freezer I can't shut it."

"You should take some to some of the older folks around town," Laine said.

"What old folks?" Ella Rae asked.

"Any of them."

Ella Rae stared at her for a moment. "So just walk up to some old guy on the street and say, 'Here's a fish'?"

That made me laugh out loud, and I think Jack chuckled as well.

"You know," Laine said, exasperated. "I don't know who the bigger smart-ass is. You or Carrigan."

"Hey now," I objected. "I believe that trophy has been awarded, and it's sitting on my mantel as we speak."

"I won't argue that," Jack grunted.

"Hahaha," I said, making a face at him.

"It would do both of you girls a world of good if you thought of someone other than yourself every now and then," Laine said.

"Here we go," I said and put my glove over my face.

"I'm serious!" she replied. "Ella Rae, how old are you?"

Ella Rae made a face. "About seventeen seconds older than you!"

I laughed. Their birthdays were three days apart.

Laine looked at me, back at Ella Rae, and then back at me and shook her head. "Never mind," she said. "There's no point in this. You both make me crazy, and this discussion is hopeless."

"I'm glad we got that settled," Ella Rae said and pulled a hand-held video game from her purse.

I laughed again, and Laine rolled her eyes.

"If I didn't know better, I'd think y'all hated each other," Jack chuckled.

"I do hate them," I said.

"Me too," Laine and Ella Rae said in unison.

Jack shook his head. "Females."

The current game was a fast, close one, and I got caught up helping Laine keep the scorebook. Jack was standing close by talking to another rancher from our parish about cattle prices, and Ella Rae was still watching Bethany Wilkes like a hawk. When Ella Rae seized onto something, neither hell nor high water could keep her from pursuing it.

The day dwindled into sunset, and the ballpark lights popped on. Bethany, according to Ella Rae, had finally talked all the makeup off her face and had left. We then had a fifteen-minute conversation about Bethany's lack of using the bathroom. Ella Rae was convinced that Bethany was a vampire. "Smooth white skin, perfect teeth, perfect body, doesn't pee. What the hell?" Ridiculous, I know, but sometimes you just had to go along with Ella Rae.

Jack never strayed too far from us after his escape from Red Claws. I wondered what that was about. Of course, he had always attended softball tournaments when we were playing, but my mind worked double overtime these days, and I was sure he had some ulterior motive. But I secretly hoped that his presence under the umbrella with me had thrown a major kink in Bethany's plans. I had caught her looking at us earlier, so I briefly laid my head on Jack's shoulder. I wasn't sure which of us was more surprised, Jack, Ella Rae, Bethany, or me. But I hadn't fooled Laine for a second. She rolled her eyes and mouthed, "You are the devil." I stuck my tongue out at her behind Jack's back and laughed a little bit too loud.

Luckily, Miss Lucy Grimes had picked that exact moment to spit her chewing tobacco at that little Thompson child, King. Miss Lucy was as mean as a snake. That sounds bad, I know, but everybody in town knew Miss Lucy didn't have any kids and didn't like any kids. Besides, that child was the devil's minion, no doubt carrying some deep psychological scars over his name. I don't know how his mama still had hair. I would've pulled mine out long ago.

I was bone tired by the time the last game rolled around. There were only about thirty people left at the park, and most of them were asleep in their cars, waiting for their players. When it was just about time to go home, my phone vibrated for what seemed like the one-hundredth time. It was last night's Greek god. Again. He'd been blowing up my phone all day even though I had made it clear to him I couldn't talk today. But that hadn't deterred him in the least. Not even the text I sent that said, "DO NOT CALL ME TODAY. PLEASE." I had even turned my phone off for a while, but when I powered up again, I had eight more messages from him. I winced as I read each one. He probably wasn't going to win a spelling bee anytime soon. The only messages I sent back were those asking him not to text me again, which he obviously either didn't understand or just ignored. So I don't know why I was surprised when I saw his his car pull up in the parking lot near midnight. Ella Rae, as only she could, summed up the situation in two words. "Oh shit!"

Chapter 3

"Jack, will you take Ella Rae home?" I asked in a slight panic but trying awfully hard to seem normal. "She rode with me, but I'm gonna help Laine pack all her stuff after the game."

"Sure," Jack said. "Whenever she's ready."

Ella Rae caught on immediately. A little too well. "Oh shit!" she said again, looking at an imaginary watch on her wrist. "Will you look at the time? I had no idea it was this late! I should've been gone hours ago! Let's go now! Here, Jack, take this for me." She was talking fast and moving faster. She began piling anything she could find in his arms—bats, bags, pillows, even the one I was sitting on. He could barely see over the top of the heap.

I scanned the parking lot for Adonis. Thankfully, he was still sitting in his car, staring intently at the little scene developing under the umbrella. Surely he would stay put until Jack was gone. Did the man have a death wish?

"Goodnight, girls!" Ella Rae said cheerfully as she corralled Jack toward his truck. "Jack, I just love your truck! I wish you'd sell it to Tommy when you get ready for a new one. I don't know why he wants to buy a Ford. I just love Chevys. What do you think about a Ford? Not too much, huh?" She was babbling nonstop.

"Good-bye, Laine," Jack called over his shoulder. "I'll see you shortly, Carrigan?"

"Yes, yes," I said. "Soon as we can leave."

"Anyway, I do love a Chevy, and I think I want a blue truck next time." Ella Rae continued talking ninety to nothing. Even when they drove away, I could still see her lips moving. Talk about a wingman!

Laine hadn't said a word during the whole scene except to tell Jack good-bye. She finally looked and me and said, "You wanna tell me what all that was about?"

I sure as hell didn't want to tell her, but I knew there was no way around it. Grimacing, I said, "Look in the parking lot to your left."

"Oh my God!" She shouted loud enough that several men whipped their heads around.

"Snake!" I shouted and began dancing around the quilt. Big mistake. Every man still standing rushed to our rescue. Laine put her feet up in her chair while they stomped and shook the quilt. She stared at me, shaking her head.

There was much discussion among the men about the species of the snake they'd successfully saved us from. Some said rattlesnake, some said cottonmouth. Too bad it had been a member of the invisible family. I thanked them profusely.

"You are one lie away from a fiery hell, Carrigan," Laine said as the snake chasers walked away.

"Still?" I asked, trying to make her laugh. Didn't work.

"Why is that man in the parking lot?" she asked, calmly scratching her pencil in the scorebook as a run scored.

"I don't know. I have texted him fifty times telling him to leave me alone today."

"So you're still assuming he can *read*," she said through slightly grit teeth. "Did you think he was going to abide by that? If you told him not to text but didn't tell him not to come, what did you think he was gonna do? I am not going to help fix this, you hear me? This is your baby to rock, your wagon to pull, and your cup of tea."

Oh hell, she had started speaking in clichés now. I may never get her to stop. "I am texting him again now. I have it all under control."

"Let me count the times I have heard *that* statement come from your lips." She sighed. "I hope you really do have it under control this time because these are your eggs and your basket."

I made a face. What the hell did that even mean? I started to point out that it made no sense, but I let her have it. "Okay," I said, pushing the send button on my phone. "I sent him a message that said to go home, I couldn't talk, and that I would call him tomorrow. You happy?"

"I'm sure it will take him ten minutes to read it," she said, tapping her pencil on the scorebook in her lap. "I hope you also told him to start the car and put it in reverse. I don't think he's bright enough to figure that out."

"Har har," I said.

"What do you always say? I calls 'em like I sees 'em?"

I ignored her. "See, he's reading it. I can tell."

"It was two sentences, Carrigan," she retorted. "How long could it take? I hope you aren't planning on having children with this man."

"Did you really just say that?"

"Are you really thinking about marrying him?" she asked, her gaze even with mine.

I ignored that too. "See, he's leaving."

"Good! And I hope he never comes back."

She may as well have thrown a bucket of scalding water on me. "What is your problem?" I demanded, probably a little louder and harsher than I had intended. "Why don't you want me to be happy?"

Laine sighed and shook her head slowly. "Carrigan," she said, her voice softer now. "All I have ever wanted was for you to be happy. That man is not going to make you happy." She sighed again. "You can never seem to see the forest for the trees."

"What I *can* see is how happy Jack is making me," I said, my eyes now hot with tears although that was an unusual development for me. I knew it was a ridiculous reaction, but I couldn't help it. I blinked hard in an effort to keep anyone, least of all Laine, from noticing.

Laine opened her mouth again to respond but then promptly shut up. After a few seconds, she said, "This isn't the time or the place."

Finally, we agreed on something. This certainly was *not* the time or the place. I began packing our things since the final game was almost over. "I'm gonna take your things to your car," I told her.

"Thank you," she said tersely and concentrated on the scorebook.

I knew I shouldn't have bitten Laine's head off, but she should be on my side, dammit! Why wasn't she ever on my side when it came to Jack? She'd defend me in front of the devil himself, but when it came to Jack, she was a brick wall. It frustrated the hell out of me. First of all, why did she think she was in a position to give me or anybody else relationship advice? She knew just as much about heart surgery. If I wanted advice about my love life, I would certainly ask somebody who had one. And I was about one more conversation like we had tonight away from telling her so. But I knew I would hurt her feelings if I did. Laine was kind, gentle, and loving. I was loud, suspicious, and headstrong. My method of delivery wasn't always what it should be. In my heart, Laine was my sister in every sense of the word. The only thing missing was the mutual blood. Those things kept me from speaking to her the same way I spoke to the rest of the world.

But I couldn't let this go on much longer. I didn't want our differences about Jack to drive a permanent wedge between us, and my resentment grew every time we had a conversation about it. I didn't expect her to endorse my extracurricular activities and was stunned that she'd agreed to take me to meet Adonis last night. Although, I did realize later it was strictly so she could keep her finger on me. She knew I was going with or without her, so she had saddled up. Probably afraid I would leave the country with him if she hadn't. In all the years Laine, Ella Rae, and I had been friends, we had never held things back from each other, and it wasn't that I wanted her to do so now. I just wanted her to tell me *why*. Why she insisted that my life was so much better in a marriage that had turned into a mere tolerance of each other. But the only response I ever got was "Jack loves you, and you love him. Don't screw this up." That was no answer. It was an opinion. I needed evidence. Laine couldn't produce it, and Jack wouldn't produce it. Laine and I were headed into a knock-down, drag-out, hide-the-kids-in-the-barn fight, and I knew it was coming. I just hoped it didn't take place where the entire world could witness it.

The tournament finally ended. We packed the rest of our things and headed to our cars. After a few brief "good nights" to the folks still there, we headed home. I watched Laine turn into her driveway. She entered the side door and waved.

Jack's truck was home, so I knew he was inside. At least he wasn't in confrontation mode tonight. Hopefully. I peered into the window from the front porch. He was on the sofa, asleep. Wow. This was a new development in the case. No matter how bad things had gotten between us, we'd always slept in the same bed. My heart sank a little. *Maybe spending half the day with Bethany had made me unappealing to him.* Dear Lord, where had *that* thought come from? I had never been insecure before, and I didn't care for the way it made me feel. I didn't want to be that wife—you know the ones. Always wondering where their man is, who he is talking to, what he is doing. Clingy. Dependent. Anxious. I couldn't be that girl; no way could I be that girl. But this marriage had begun turning me into her, and I hated and resented it.

I sat down in the porch swing and laid my head on the pillow. I just couldn't bring myself to go inside yet. I didn't want to wake him up. I didn't want a conversation or a confrontation about sleeping arrangements, Bethany, me, him, any of it. I just wanted to be still for a little while. It seemed as though my life was becoming a constant torrent of emotions, a never-ending barrage of peaks and valleys. The things that had excited me were beginning to annoy me, and the things that annoyed me I found myself fantasizing about. What a mess.

My phone suddenly vibrated, and I jumped and then rolled my eyes. If it was Adonis again, I was going to kill him myself. But it was Ella Rae, dying to know what had happened after she'd left with Jack. She was texting me from the bathroom closet so Tommy wouldn't hear her. That made me laugh. I knew her husband loved me. Like the rest of us, we'd known each other our entire lives. But I also knew that my clandestine affairs bothered him. I knew Ella Rae had told him about Adonis and the one before him. She told Tommy everything. She even told us she was going to. She was so in love with Tommy, I swear they breathed in unison. And Tommy was just as bad. I don't know how he functioned when she wasn't right beside him. They had started liking each other when we were in the eighth grade and Tommy was a freshman. They'd been together ever since and were the perfect match. I had wished a thousand times my own marriage was like theirs.

My phone buzzed again. I smiled at her sad face icon and dialed her number.

Chapter 4

Summer was definitely upon us in Bon Dieu Falls. It was only the end of May, but the temperatures had already soared to the upper nineties in the afternoons. The humidity had shown up already too. I kept my hair in a French braid most of the time because fixing it was useless. Besides, it was too long and too thick to wear down. I had inherited my grandmother's auburn hair and my mother's texture. When big hair came back in style, I would be ready.

The hair issue kept most of the self-proclaimed Southern belles I knew indoors during the day. That was a little amusing to me. You missed everything if you were locked up all the time. But they didn't want to look a mess, and the heat made them feel faint. I filed these women away under "weak." Weak women both annoyed and amused me.

School had let out for the summer that day, and I was very excited about that. Laine was a teacher at the junior high, and I loved it when she was home every day instead of working. It meant she, Ella Rae, and I could spend our days together. Ella Rae was a housewife, and I was … Carrigan. Oh, I had a job in the office at Whitfield Farms; I just didn't attend it regularly. It was a made-up job anyway—entering information on the cattle into the computer. Jack had designed it to keep me busy. I had agreed to it, but it had gotten really old, really fast. Even though I truly loved the farm, sitting at a desk all day made me feel like a caged animal. I think Jack had ultimately hoped I would turn into a domesticated Ella Rae who kept a spotless house, had supper on the table at six p.m. sharp every night, and had a happy husband. Well, one out of three wasn't bad. Juanita Johnson kept my house spic and span.

I looked out the window again, checking to see if Laine had made it home from school. I wanted her and Ella Rae to go to Shreveport with me to shop today. The annual crawfish boil at Whitfield Farms was this weekend, and I needed a new outfit. I knew Bethany Wilkes would be there in all her glory, and there was no way I was going to let that pasty-faced swizzle stick outshine me again. She would no doubt have her missiles on display and wearing God only knew what on her feet. I had to find something spectacular, although I was a fan of wearing my boobies *inside* my shirt. I needed Ella Rae and Laine to help because they didn't keep their opinions a secret. In fact, they would gag, laugh, and point if they didn't like something. Good thing I wasn't sensitive. I dialed Laine's number again, but still no answer.

I noticed a missed call on my phone. It was the Greek god. Again. A month had passed since the first time I'd met him in Shreveport, and I had met him once more after that. But I had recently come to the conclusion that the sneaking around was much better than actually being with him. He was, in fact, an idiot. He wasn't even really good in bed, and after we were done, there was absolutely nothing to talk about. I finally told him the last time to not talk at all. I hated to admit to Laine that she'd been right, but I did. She was both elated and smug about the admission and gave me the whole speech about not doing anything stupid like this anymore and how I could now concentrate on my marriage and maybe think about starting a family. Poor Laine. She saw life through all those romance novels she always had her nose stuck in. But she had no idea how the real world worked. Still, I shook my head in all the right places and let her talk. It made her so happy to think that I had come to my senses.

I texted Adonis and told him for the umpteenth time that it was over between us. I had a little bit of guilt about the whole situation. Not because of Jack. I'd only done to him what he'd done to me. But it had been wrong to use Adonis like I had. He was a good guy, and I could give him the highest of all southern compliments, which was he had a good heart. Besides, Adonis didn't love me; he only thought he did. And I didn't love him either, although I had told him on a couple occasions I did. He would make someone a good husband, but not me. It just wasn't there. He'd get over it. The only thing really good between us was the flirting. And it was fun to be chased again.

The truth was, I missed Jack. Correction. I missed what life used to be like with Jack, and that was what I was searching for. What a sobering thought. One I had no idea how to pursue or even if I wanted to pursue it at all. I wasn't going to fling myself at a man who no longer wanted me. I had my pride, and I intended to keep it.

I wished for the millionth time I could put my finger on what had gone wrong. When had it all gone south? We had been so happy. At least I had been. But a couple years ago, Jack just sort of pulled away from me. Nothing massive, just noticeable. I didn't press him for details at the time. I just figured he needed his space. But weeks turned into months, and months turned into two years. And now we were in a Mexican standoff, and I wasn't going to be the first to blink. Damn Jack, anyway. This was all his fault. If he would have kept his pants zipped, I would have too.

Laine popped in the front door, scaring me to death.

"Damn, girl, you scared me!" I said.

"Guilty conscience?" she asked and winked.

"Ha, ha!" I said. "I've been calling you for thirty minutes. Where have you been?"

"Ugh, school," she said and plopped down on the sofa. "I am exhausted."

"From what? You were there forty-five seconds!"

"I'm still tired," she complained. "I was up half the night."

"Why?" Laine was a ten-o'clock girl most nights.

"*A Star Is Born* was on." She smiled.

I rolled my eyes. "Girl, you need to step out of la-la land and find you a man! Now go on home, change clothes, and splash some water on your face. We're going to Shreveport for new clothes. Woohoo!"

"Ugh!" she said. "Not today!"

"Yes, today!" I said. "There are only three shopping days left till crawfish time. I'm under incredible pressure! I have to look stunning."

"Ugh," she said again and buried her head in the pillow.

"Now go on. Scoot! I'm not about to look like I just jumped off of *Cows Weekly* while Bethany Wilkes looks like she's been on the red carpet."

"You are crazy," Laine said. "Jack does not want Bethany Wilkes. And I do not want to go to Shreveport."

"Too bad," I said. "We're all going. Ella Rae is on her way, so we'll pick you up shortly."

"Crap!" she said, dragging herself off the sofa in the dramatic way only she could. She walked to the door, muttering her favorite phrases. "I can't believe y'all are making me go. I never get to just stay home. It's always something."

"See you in a few!" I called after her as she closed the door.

Laine could bitch and moan all she wanted, but the truth was, if Ella Rae and I were going somewhere or doing something, Laine wanted to be there too. She may hate the activity, but she was going. She'd screamed at us while we skinny-dipped in the creek, she'd frog hunted with us, ran yoyos with us, sat in Tiger Stadium with cotton in her ears, and sat in the car and shook her head while we danced on the side of the road to a favorite song. I watched her drag herself across the road and suddenly thought of a night years ago, the night of my twenty-first birthday to be exact. The memory made me laugh out loud. It always did.

Jack and the girls had thrown me a big birthday bash at the country club in Natchitoches. All our friends were there, and the party had been a blast. But later in the evening, after I'd had a little too much to drink, I decided to confront a woman Jack used to date. Lexi Carter had shown up just before midnight, uninvited and unwelcome. Jack was dating her right before he and I had gotten together. Hell, Jack had dated *everybody* except Laine and Ella Rae before we got together. But the fact that he'd dated her wasn't what bothered me. I couldn't very well stay mad at half the women I knew. But he'd stayed with Lexi longer than he had stayed with most girls. In fact, everyone in town assumed he would marry her, myself included.

The thing that really made me want to spit nails about Lexi was a letter she'd written to Jack right after he and I got married. In it, she had expressed her undying love and affection for him and promised to wait for him until he was over his infatuation with me. But the last line of that letter was burned into my mind like a tattoo. "Call me when your little girl gets done playing house." Jack had to almost sit on me to keep me from going to find her. I was infuriated. Worse than infuriated. I couldn't say her name without wanting to spit afterward. Jack had assured me over and over again there was nothing left between them, that he'd never really loved her at all. He told me he never wanted secrets between us, and that's why he gave me the letter in the first place. I eventually believed him. I knew he was telling me the truth. Nobody could fake a love like we had going on during the first few years of our marriage. We were solid. But seeing her at my birthday party had been like pouring gasoline on a smoldering fire. Jack and I had been married almost four years by then, but the memory of that letter had never faded. Looking back, I may have let it go had she just made a brief appearance and then left the same way she came in. But as the evening wore on, she inched her way closer to Jack, and I'd been pretty chummy with Jack Daniels all night. That combination just was not good.

"I'm going to talk to her," I finally told Laine and Ella Rae.

Ella Rae, always my biggest cheerleader, had been chomping at the bit for a confrontation all night. "Hell yes you're going to talk to her! And I'm gonna talk to that bitch too!"

"Neither of you are going to do any such thing!" Laine scolded. "You are going to act like a lady, Carrigan, and you are going to shut up, Ella Rae!"

"Who you talking to?" Ella Rae asked, startled. She'd shared my affection for Jack Daniels all night.

Laine put her arm around Ella Rae and explained to her why ladies don't confront people and that she was going to make ladies out of both of us one day. I knew that discussion could last for hours, so I took the opportunity to escape. By the time they realized I was gone, I was standing right in front of Lexi Carter.

Jack must've seen it coming because he was by my side in an instant. "How's my birthday girl?" he said, sliding his arm around my waist.

I shoved his hand. "Get off me, Jack," I said and then looked at Lexi.

"Why are you here?" I asked her. I felt Laine's hand on one arm and Ella Rae's on the other. Didn't take them long to show up.

She smiled at me, and if I hadn't been furious and my adrenaline wasn't pumping at a hundred miles per hour, the red lipstick on her caps would've been hilarious. "Now, Carri," she said reaching for me. "Haven't we buried the hatchet, sweetheart?"

Two problems with that answer actually. One, she'd called me "Carri," which was reserved only for those closest to me, and two, she'd been condescending. "Sweetheart?" Seriously? She may as well have thrown a drink in my face. I was drunk, I was mad, and I was twenty-one. That combination was worse than Ella Rae, Jack Daniels, and me.

"I tell you what we can bury, Lexi," I said, my hands on my hips. "We can bury you're ass—" Jack caught me around the waist again and was trying to pull me away.

Laine walked over to Lexi and told her something I couldn't hear. Whatever it was, it didn't appear to make a difference.

"If Carri wants me to leave, she can ask me to leave," Lexi said.

"I want you to leave. You weren't invited, and I don't want you here. So good-bye," I said. There ... that oughta cover it. Jack released his hold a little.

"What's wrong, Carri?" Lexi smiled and looked Jack up and down. "You afraid of a little competition?"

"You gotta be shitting me!" I yelled, ready to pounce.

"Lexi!" Jack said, "Get out of here! Now!"

"Still can't control her, Jack?" Lexi kept smiling.

I didn't have time to react, and neither did Jack. All I heard was Ella Rae's loud protest, "Oh *hell* no!" and the pop of a fist connecting with a jaw. Only Lexi had ducked, and Ella Rae had landed an impressive right hook square on Laine's cheek. It was one of the few times I ever heard Laine really curse.

"Son of a bitch! Son of a *bitch*!" Laine danced around, holding her cheek.

"Oh shit! Oh, Laine, I'm so sorry!" Ella Rae said, trying to assess the damage she'd done. But Laine wouldn't have it. She wouldn't let Ella Rae or me anywhere near her.

Jack had taken over in an instant. "Lexi, I told you once to get out, now leave! Tommy, please take Carrigan with you and Ella Rae. I'm taking Laine home."

Jack had ushered Laine out the door immediately while the rest of us stood there a little sheepishly. Tommy handled the situation in his laid-back way. "Come on, y'all. It ain't a party till somebody gets a black eye. Nice jab, baby." He patted Ella Rae on her backside. The crowd rippled a little nervous laughter, and the music started again.

We left the party right behind Jack and Laine, and when we got to her house, she refused to talk to Ella Rae or me. In fact, it had taken her a week to speak to us at all. And you couldn't really call it speaking. She ranted. She raved. She lectured. All Ella Rae and I could do was take it. Ella Rae had given Laine her first shiner, and I had started the whole mess. Not to mention, Laine was always mortified at being part of any sort of scandal. She asked us repeatedly what we wanted her to tell her students. That Miss Landry was in a drunken brawl at the country club? That made Ella Rae and me laugh, and that really started some fallout. Laine told us we were immature and irresponsible, and that it was time to put away childish things. I was pretty sure the preacher had said the same thing from the pulpit, but if she wanted to preach, who was I to stop her?

Laine lectured for at least forty-five minutes before Ella Rae or I got a word in. It was hard to look at her too. Ella Rae had knocked the *hell* out of her. I had never had a black eye like that, and I had played some type of sport my entire life. I wanted to tell her how impressed I was, and then thought I should just leave it alone. But anytime she turned her back to us, Ella Rae would whisper, "Did you see her eye? Oh my God! I didn't know I could do that!" Ella Rae really did feel awful about hitting her, but she was like me. We'd both had knee surgeries, broken fingers, busted lips, stitches, you name it. All this commotion over a black eye seemed ridiculous. But this was Laine we were talking about, and she was a girlie girl.

By the time the fight story had circulated Bon Dieu Falls a time or two, I had broken Lexi's arm, cracked two of her ribs, and rearranged her face enough that she needed plastic surgery. And I had never even touched her. Ah, life in a small town.

Lexi left the parish shortly after that. I never knew exactly where she went, but the rumor was that she'd moved to New Orleans. I was sure she'd become a call girl and a cheap one at that. Okay, that's just the catty female coming out in me, but I enjoyed the fantasy. In fact, I didn't see her again until about two years ago. I drove up to the post office one morning, and there she was. I sat in my car and watched as she got into hers. Why was she here? Was she checking her mail? Had she moved back?

I called Ella Rae immediately. She had heard nothing about Lexi Carter. I texted Laine at school. She didn't know anything either. I called Jack at the farm next. I acted like it was a casual call and was just asking how his day was going. We used to do that quite a bit. Finally, I mentioned that I had seen Lexi and asked him if he knew she was in town. He said somebody had told him she'd moved back, but he hadn't seen her. The fact that he knew she was back and hadn't told me annoyed me, but I didn't let on. But that night was the first time I noticed there was distance between us. It didn't take me long to put two and two together. Eventually, I asked him if he'd been seeing her, but of course, he denied it. I tried every way in the world to catch him. I followed him sometimes and went through his wallet, phone, truck, and receipts. I never found any evidence, but there was *something* wrong at my house, and I was crushed. I was completely, absolutely, and totally in love with Jack Whitfield III. And until Lexi had moved back, my marriage had been happy, loving, and unwavering.

Then, about six months after she'd shown up, Lexi disappeared just as quickly. I was elated, hoping against hope that her absence would bring Jack's presence back to me. Nevertheless, my husband was still withdrawn and reserved, but only when we were alone. I supposed he needed to keep up appearances; after all, we had to keep that Whitfield name shiny. Sometime after, and I can't even tell you when it happened, my despair turned into defiance, and I just stopped trying. If he was going to do this crap to me, I would certainly give it back. Enter Adonis number one ...

The sound of Ella Rae's screeching tires yanked me from my trip down memory lane. The girl drove like a bat out of hell. Always had. I shook my head in an effort to clear the unpleasant memories and grabbed my purse.

Chapter 5

The morning of the crawfish boil broke bright and beautiful. The weather was perfect, albeit a little warm. I was going to the farm early, and the girls were going with me. Jack had left around six a.m. and had actually kissed my forehead while I faked sleep. That had surprised me, but I didn't open my eyes. Where had this come from? He had begun being a little more affectionate lately, and it annoyed, pleased, and confused me. Why now, when I had clearly crossed a line in our marriage? I sighed. How had my life gotten this complicated? I compartmentalized the thought and got in the shower.

The farm was already buzzing with life when we arrived around ten a.m. The party didn't officially start until four but that had never stopped anybody yet. It was always like this. People started arriving before noon and left after midnight. Another reason I would never leave Bon Dieu Falls, although I knew there were certainly places more exciting, was that I knew these people, I mean, really knew them. I knew Bobby Ray Curtis would get drunk and hit on me tonight but not mean a thing by it. In the big city, they called that sexual harassment, but in Bon Dieu Falls, we called it "Bobby Ray Curtis got drunk and hit on me last night." I knew Jeannie McMillian would get mad at her husband around noon today and stay mad at him until they left tonight. I knew Jamie Washington would hug me so tight my ribs would almost crack and tell me he still remembered when we were in first grade and I slapped him for using my purple crayon and we'd rolled on the floor and fought till our teacher broke us up. People could say what they wanted about small towns, but I could call just about anybody I knew, black or white, and they would show up if I needed them. Any time of the day or night. Yep, these were *my* people. The black ones, the white ones, the old ones, and the young ones. You couldn't drag me out of this town.

I made the rounds like a good Whitfield and talked to my in-laws and my parents before catching up with Ella Rae and Laine. I found them under the largest oak tree in the yard. Several of our friends had gathered there and were in the middle of a pretty hot game of horseshoes. I squeezed between the girls in the tree swing, only to pop right back up when I saw a familiar face.

"There you are!" Charlotte Freeman reached out to hug me. "I've been looking for you all morning! Where have you been?"

I hugged her back. It was so good to see her. I had always liked Charlotte. She was a couple of years older than Ella Rae, Laine, and me, but we had spent a lot of time with her in high school. In fact, after my girls, Charlotte was about the only other female I really trusted. That hadn't changed since she'd gone off to LSU and married what we in Bon Dieu Falls called a foreign boy—he was from Mississippi. She and her husband came from Vicksburg every year to the crawfish boil. Charlotte had proven time and time again to be a true and trusted friend, and I was genuinely glad to see her.

"I've been keeping a low profile," I laughed.

She raised her brow. "I find that hard to believe. You look fantastic! And so tiny!"

I made a face. "I'm starving myself," I confessed. "I haven't had anything that tasted good in two weeks."

"Because?" Charlotte asked.

I rolled my eyes. "Bethany Wilkes, the porcelain princess."

"Oh please!" Charlotte said. "I have heels higher than her standards! Is she still sniffing around? And is she still having shoe issues?"

"Worse than ever," I said. "On both counts."

"I don't know why in the world you would ever give her a second thought," Charlotte said and made a face as though the thought left a bad taste in her mouth. "Jack doesn't want Bethany Wilkes."

"And you base this psychic knowledge on what?"

"On the fact that you're ten times prettier, smarter, and funnier than she is," Charlotte said. "Not to mention that the man married *you*."

I shook my head. "I just don't know what to think anymore, Charlotte. Besides, I have … crossed a line." I looked at her to see if she understood.

She did. Right away. "Oh, honey, you didn't."

It was maybe the first time I really felt bad about cheating on Jack. It suddenly seemed so … wrong. "I just … I don't know. It seemed like the thing to do at the time."

"What a completely stupid reason," Charlotte said.

At least that made me laugh.

"Is this a full-blown affair or just a fling?" she asked.

"Just a fling. And it's over."

"That's good." She pursed her lips in thought. "Look, Carri, you know your husband better than anyone else. And I'm not saying something isn't wrong. I just don't think it's about another woman. I never have."

I had never wanted to believe that either. But how could I deny it? It was just like he had flipped a switch. One day we were happy, the next day he was cold. And it happened when Lexi Carter rolled back into town. It was true that I'd never had any solid evidence that Jack was cheating on me. But I had a feeling. Some nagging, annoying suspicion I couldn't shake or make sense of. What the hell else could it be?

"Trust me on this one, Carri," Charlotte reiterated. "I just don't believe it's another woman. And I know Ella Rae thinks he's cheating too, but she only believes it because you do. If you said you saw Elvis in the garden at the cemetery, Ella Rae would say, 'And he was singing "Hound Dog"!' But fifty bucks says you haven't sold Laine on the idea."

"Oh, you are right about that," I said. "Laine could see a video of him with another woman and swear in court it was fake."

Charlotte and I looked at Ella Rae and Laine still in the tree swing, watching Tommy give Jimmy Dreison a solid whipping at horseshoes. Ella Rae was cheering while Laine looked on, smiling.

"And speaking of Laine, what have y'all done to her?" Charlotte asked.

"What do you mean?"

"She looks terrible. Like she hasn't slept in a week."

I hadn't noticed it until now, but Laine really did look bad. She looked tired. She'd been working day and night on a project for Bible school, which was coming up the next week at the First Baptist Church we all attended. Some of us more than others. Laine was there every time the doors were open. Ella Rae and I were mostly Sunday-morning Christians.

"You know Laine," I said. "She's working on something for Bible school, and it has to be perfect, so she probably really hasn't slept in a week."

"Maybe so," Charlotte mused. "But she sure looks like she could use some rest."

I studied Laine. She just looked like she needed some sleep to me. But I made a mental note to ask her later if she felt alright.

The horseshoe match got loud about then, and Charlotte and I joined the cheering.

There were a dozen different activities going on under the massive oaks at Whitfield Farms. The older folks enjoyed Bouré games, horseshoes, dominoes, and Spades in the shady backyard while the younger crowd gathered in front to play volleyball. A little petting zoo had been set up at the barn for the little ones, and most every tween in town was either in or around the pool or the waterslide. A local band provided music, and Mr. Jack had gotten a couple of ranch hands to build a wooden dance floor under the oaks. There were at least three hundred people in attendance, including three senators and the governor himself, who had gone to college with my daddy and Jack's daddy as well.

The party was in full swing by four p.m., and I had officially been on my best behavior all day. I hadn't had anything stronger than water to drink and had even turned down the sissified mint julep Jack's mother had offered me earlier. No use in tempting fate. Bethany had arrived, fashionably late, and looking like a million bucks. Except for those wooden salad bowls on her feet. I knew from the instant irritation I felt looking at her that I'd be on straight water the rest of the day or she would be on her ass by the end of the night. Thankfully, Jack was so busy talking about football, cattle, soybeans, and politics all day—pretty much the only four things Louisiana men talked about—that he'd never even noticed Bethany. I knew because I had watched him. All day. It was exhausting but necessary when half the women in town would give their great-grandmother's china to be in your shoes.

I had seen very little of Ella Rae and Laine all day. I had eaten crawfish with them earlier, but since my last name was Whitfield, I was part of the hostess regime. Ella Rae had spent most of the day playing volleyball. Poor thing was as competitive as I was. We sometimes stayed up all night long playing Yahtzee because neither of us would quit if we were behind.

Laine was under one of the big white tents entertaining everybody's kids with face painting and games. Children thought she was the original Mother Goose. I wished she would have a baby of her own, and I encouraged that all the time. But she was completely mortified at the thought. "I'm not married! I don't even have a boyfriend!" I pointed out on several occasions that a husband or boyfriend was not a requirement for having a baby and assured her that if she was uncomfortable with the one-night-stand route, she could go the turkey-baster route. I thought she was going to pass out discussing it. She'd made me promise to go to church the next Sunday just for suggesting she have a "baster baby out of wedlock." Needless to say, she was neither amused nor interested. But she begged Ella Rae and me to have a baby so she could take care of it. But Ella Rae wasn't about to give birth to anything that kept her off a softball field or a tennis court, and the last thing I needed to add to my messed-up house was a baby. Besides, my sister had three kids, and I hadn't held the first one until their heads had stopped flopping around. Little babies scared the hell out of me.

The crawfish boil was, once again, a huge success and loads of fun. It had really been a good day. I was so excited to see several friends who no longer lived here but always came down to attend the boil. Especially Charlotte. We talked on the phone once or twice a month, but there was no substitute for actually seeing a friend in person. Even her Mississippi husband had begun to grow on me a little. They left promising to meet us at LSU in the fall for a football tailgate.

I pondered what Charlotte and I had talked about on and off all day. Even though some part of me wanted to believe her, how could I let myself? But she was right. I knew my husband better than anyone.

And I knew something was wrong and had been for a long time. It *had* to be about another woman. How could it be anything else? But why wouldn't he just ask me for a divorce and be done with it? I'd signed a prenuptial agreement, so he wasn't going to lose a dime. Besides, if he was fooling around, I didn't want to stay with him. I'd only cheated on him because I thought he was cheating on me. So if I ever found out he had, I could say, "Oh yeah? Well, guess what?" But I'll be damned if I were going to end up like Nancy Wheeler whose husband's affairs were so common, the man was virtually scandal proof. I swear if he drove up to the bank with two hookers and a circus clown, nobody would even blink an eye. We'd probably all think, *Oh, poor Nancy*, and go back about our business. No, I didn't want to be the next Nancy Wheeler. I'd rather have my information right between the eyes.

I had no idea what was going on with Jack, but one thing was certain. He'd been a saint today. In fact, today he'd been the Jack I married eleven years ago. Very loving, attentive, and present. But I understood it was just a show for today's audience, and it made me confused and sad.

Chapter 6

*J*uly was hotter than any I could remember. It also found the girls and me busier than any other summer. Ella Rae's mother had just had knee replacement surgery, so she'd gone to Shreveport to help her until she could literally get back on her feet. Laine had accepted a position teaching summer school, so she tutored high school kids four nights a week. We'd hardly seen each other at all since the crawfish boil.

And I was going to be at the farm with Jack. His parents had gone on a month-long cruise, so Jack had to be there to deal with the day-to-day operations. There was no way I was going to let him go by himself. Things may have been strained between us, but I wasn't going to add fuel to the fire by staying in town. Although I heard the speculation about the state of our marriage was pretty much split down the middle in Bon Dieu Falls. Half the town was betting on divorce, and the other half said we'd always stay together. It always stunned me when somebody shared that kind of crap with me. What was I supposed to say to that? It took me a very long time to realize that I didn't have to say anything at all. There was no sense in running around town, putting out fires or sweeping up speculation. Charlotte had put that in perspective for me when she said, "Honey, if they aren't sleeping in your bed or paying your bills, whatever you do is none of their damn business."

It had taken years for Diane Whitfield to talk Jack Whitfield Jr. into taking this Mediterranean cruise. He'd always found every excuse in the world not to go, but after forty years of marriage, he'd run out of ammunition. They had left early this morning. I had never seen Mrs. Diane so excited or Mr. Jack more apprehensive. It was pretty amusing. Mr. Jack had spent at least an hour going over the same things he'd told Jack the day before. He always did that. I asked Jack once if it annoyed him, and he had just smiled. "Just who he is," he said. It would have annoyed the hell out of me but very little bothered Jack. I loved Mr. Jack, but sometimes I wanted to ask him, "Who do you think took care of this place while you recovered from heart surgery five years ago?" But I kept my mouth shut.

Jack was a great deal like his father in other ways, though. They were both fairly quiet and reserved. But when they spoke, it was significant. They were polite and reflective, but there was never any doubt about who was in charge if either of them were present. It never failed to leave me in awe. It wasn't just their physical presence either, although they were both big men, over six feet tall. It was an aura that followed them, an attitude, the way they carried themselves that was both natural and mystic. Watching them handle different situations over the years had dropped my jaw on more than one occasion. The fact that either of them could have bought and sold this town anytime they chose yet were the first in line to help a neighbor made them all the more an enigma.

Mrs. Diane had asked me to ride her horse, Gilda, every day while she was away, and I was looking forward to it. She had been quite the accomplished rider in her younger days and had won competitions all over the southeast. When she'd married Mr. Jack, she'd given it all up to help him start the farm and raise their only child, my husband. I had often wondered if there had been a time she ever resented giving up everything and moving from her home state of Tennessee to move here with him where she knew no one. But one day, as she was showing me some of her trophies and ribbons in the library of their home, I asked her if she felt like she'd missed out on anything.

"It was a wonderful time in my life, but no. I am exactly where I want to be." I adored her, almost as much as I adored my own mother. Mrs. Diane had welcomed me into this family with open arms and an open mind, even though I had married her only child when I seventeen years old. Looking back, I knew they surely had concerns over that. But they had never voiced them to me or to Jack. All I had found here was love and acceptance. In fact, when I had cheated on Jack, it was the thought of his parents, not him, that made me feel guilty.

The farm was only fifteen minutes out of Bon Dieu Falls, but when you were here, it felt like a different and all-inclusive world. I liked being at the farm. I liked lazing in the big wicker swing on the massive porch that wrapped around the house. I liked listening to the hired hands tell Jack about their day. I liked helping Mamie in the kitchen, although I am pretty sure she didn't like it too much. I was fairly useless in a kitchen situation, but she did let me lick the spoons every now and then. She'd been with the Whitfield's since Jack was a baby and even lived on the farm in a little house Mr. Jack had built for her. She'd known Mrs. Diane when they were both still in Tennessee and from what I could gather had run away from an abusive relationship. Nobody ever talked about that too much, and I didn't dare ask. All I knew was that Mamie wasn't interested in a man, and she loved this family like it was her own.

But I missed Laine and Ella Rae. I talked and texted with them every day, and I had repeatedly asked Laine to come out to the farm for supper, but she was always too busy. She lived for that job. I guessed all teachers must. You would have to with the things you had to put up with. I am sure I would've lasted fifteen minutes in the teaching profession. The first time one of the kids popped off at me, I'd have gone to jail. But Laine always defended them, saying that you never knew how things were in their homes or that they were just trying to find their way. Laine's mother, Jeanette Landry, had just retired from the teaching profession recently, and I knew she'd been the same kind of educator Laine was. The apple sure hadn't fallen far from that tree.

Ella Rae called one night and told me that either she or her mother would probably die that night, as she was thinking of smothering her mom in her sleep or cutting her own wrist. I laughed so hard listening to her nursing stories and her mom's antics while on pain medication that my stomach was sore. Ella Rae was supposed to stay with her for six weeks, but I didn't see how that was ever going to happen. After we hung up, I sighed. I missed my friends.

I really did love being on the farm. It was peaceful and serene, two things that weren't usually high priorities to me, but I was learning to embrace them both. However, something about this place endeared me to Jack, and I had to be really careful about that. Maybe it was because this was where it had started between us. Right here at the Whitfield's crawfish boil when I was sixteen years old. I knew who he was, of course, everybody did. But I'd never actually talked to him. He was twenty-six years old, ancient by my standards at the time. He was good-looking and charming, and I was ready. When I saw him walking in our direction, I had told Ella Rae and Laine, "Let me handle this," and they had—mainly because they had drool running down their chins.

Jack opened that encounter by leaning up against the tree we were sitting under and saying, "I believe I have stumbled upon two of the best softball players in the state and the newly elected president of the Louisiana Beta Club. Congratulations on the state championship, ladies, and on your election, Miss Landry."

Laine and Ella Rae wiggled around like praised puppies, and honestly, I was pretty shell-shocked myself. This man was exceptionally handsome up close and in person. Those blue eyes alone were enough to make a girl stupid. Thankfully, I had recovered quickly enough that I knew he hadn't noticed my control slipping. "Why, you sure have done your homework," I said.

He crossed his arms. "A blond, a brunette, and a redhead to boot? How lucky can a country boy get?" He flashed a lopsided grin.

Damn, this man had dimples too. I thought Ella Rae and Laine were going to melt into a puddle. I wasn't feeling too stable either; my heart was beating wildly in my chest. But I'll be damned if I was going to fall at his feet like every other woman seemed to.

"A country boy?" I asked. "You've been off to college in the big city and traveled all over the place. You still consider yourself a country boy?"

"Oh, I consider myself many things, darlin'," he said and winked. "Sorta like a jack-of-all-trades."

Ella Rae and Laine giggled like they were ten years old at their big sister's slumber party.

"Do you have any idea how cheesy that was?" I asked, raising my brow.

He chuckled. "Was it now?"

I could see Lexi Carter standing on the balcony of the house, watching this little scene. I turned to Jack and gestured with my eyes. "While we all appreciate this oh-so-original banter, I don't think your girlfriend is loving it."

"Hmm ..." he said, but he didn't bother turning around. Instead he leaned toward me until his face was inches from mine. If he'd gotten any closer, he would've been able to hear my heart pounding. "Tell me something, Miss Carrigan Suzanne French. Are you always this sweet?"

I sucked in my breath, willing my voice to stay even. For some ridiculous reason, when he used my entire name, I wanted to wiggle like a puppy too. But instead I swung like a champ. "Damn!" I said. "I was sweet yesterday, and you missed it!"

He pulled away and chuckled again. "Just my luck," he said. "You girls staying around awhile?"

"Probably not," I said, although I had no idea what kind of plans we had.

"Where you headed later?" he asked.

I smiled the smile I reserved for my daddy when I really wanted something bad before I answered. "You know, I think we're headed over to the National Federation of None of Your Damn Business. By the way, we're children! You could get arrested for this, you know."

He laughed in earnest and then leaned in again and shook his head. "Ms. French," he said. "I am acutely aware of just how dangerous it is for me to be around you."

There went my heart again. "We sure appreciate your hospitality," I smiled again. "But I'm afraid we need to run now. Goodnight, Mr. Whitfield."

Mercifully, the zombie girls followed me as I walked away. It was *killing* me not to turn around to see if he was still looking, but I knew it would ruin my exit. However, I could hear his low chuckle behind us, and that pleased me indeed.

Like he did most people, he intrigued me. But I hadn't really cared if he paid much attention to me or not. I had other stuff going on, including an on-again, off-again high school boyfriend, plus there were sports to play and beer to drink. But I could understand why women were so captivated by Jack, especially after the encounter at the crawfish boil. A girl would have to be dead not to appreciate that.

But it wasn't just women; men liked him too. He was extremely attractive and wealthy but acted like he was oblivious to either of those facts, which made him everybody's favorite guy. He was just as at home at a softball game in Bon Dieu Falls as he was at the governor's mansion in Baton Rouge. If the hands on the farm were fixing a fence, he wasn't in the truck watching. He and Mr. Jack were fixing the fence with them. He could drink beer with the good ole boys on Saturday night and then move mountains in the state legislature come Monday morning. He was perfect.

Only nobody was perfect. I became obsessed with finding the chink in his armor. So I started looking for it, paying closer attention when he was around. I had to be as inconspicuous as I could, though, lest he caught me watching him. Yes, it was exhausting, but bear in mind, I was seventeen and on a mission. Then one night, near the end of summer and just after my seventeenth birthday, I thought I had finally found the flaw that would certainly keep him from perfection. What I had actually done, though, was seal my fate with the man.

There was a boat landing on Red River where a lot of our friends sometimes congregated if there was nothing else going on in town that night. We were all pretty friendly with the cops around here, and they let us slide with our beer and other alcohol if we weren't too loud or too drunk or generally showing our asses. But sometimes, if there was a new cop hanging around, we fled to the boat landing for fear he'd try to flex his muscles.

There were probably fifty or sixty people there that night, and we had a pretty good party going on. I knew everybody there, excluding a couple guys who'd driven up on Harley Davidsons. We all eyed them, but they were talking to Eddie Rivers and Johnny Mac, two boys we went to school with, so they seemed harmless, and the party continued.

Sometime before midnight, I saw Jack and Lexi Carter drive up in his pickup. I watched her get out, making an unpleasant face and wiping at a speck of dirt on her shorts that favored panties instead. I was immediately annoyed. *God, am I jealous?* I rolled my eyes. At the time, I knew very little about Lexi Carter, just that she had gone to high school at Grayson, our parish rival, was a dental hygienist for some dentist in Alexandria, and dated Jack Whitfield III. None of those things endeared her to me.

She and Jack started talking to a group of people near where they'd parked. I leaned up against Parker Tillman's tailgate and observed from afar. Lexi kept her hand on Jack's arm even when she was talking to somebody else, which I found childish and stupid. Was he base or something? Jack didn't seem to notice it much, but when he had, he pulled away from her, which I found pleasing and encouraging.

"What are you staring at?" Ella Rae asked me from atop Tommy's shoulders.

"Nothing," I said and looked away from Jack and Lexi.

"Bull," Laine said from inside the truck. "She's been staring at Jack Whitfield for an hour."

"I have not! I'm just bored, is all."

"Whatever," Laine said and continued flipping through radio stations.

"Y'all wanna go climb the fire tower?" Tommy asked.

"Ugh ... please, not again." Laine groaned.

"That was only fun the first fifty times," I said.

"She doesn't want to leave here 'cause she's enjoying the view too much," Laine interjected.

I made a face at her. "For real? I'm not the one who peed my pants the last time he talked to me."

Ella Rae laughed too loud and too long at that the way she always did when she was drinking. But it was contagious, and Tommy and I laughed too.

"I did not 'pee my pants' as you so eloquently put it," Laine said. "But you have to admit it. The man *is* good looking."

"He's alright," I said as my heart quickened when he looked our way. I turned hastily toward Tommy before Jack could meet my gaze and found myself staring at a male face I didn't know.

"Is your name Carrigan?" he asked.

Wow. Don't light a match, I thought. *Pure grain alcohol breath.* "Who wants to know?" I asked.

"I'm Garrett," he said. "And I like what I see."

Where are we? Caveman days? "Is that right?" I asked, cordial but not friendly. "Well, Garrett, I'm flattered but not interested."

"Don't be like that, baby," Garrett said, leaning up against the tailgate. "I got a fine Harley over there, and I'd love to take you for a ride."

"Horrified of motorcycles," I lied. "Sorry."

"Not a pretty little spitfire like you," he said, taking a step closer. "I thought redheads liked an adventure."

"Really," I said. "I appreciate the offer, but I'm just not interested." I took a step back.

"Come on," he said and winked. "Just one little ride. Ladies like to ride on my ... bike." He laughed at his not funny joke—a drunken peal of cackles.

I could usually handle guys and their unwanted advances, but this fella was making me a little bit uncomfortable. I looked at Tommy who'd already begun to assess the situation and was helping Ella Rae off his shoulders.

"Look, man," Tommy said to him. "She already told you she ain't interested."

"Who the hell are you?" Garrett asked. "Her husband?"

Tommy put his hand on my shoulder. "Yeah, I am," he said. "We just don't like to talk about it much."

"Man, back off," Garrett said and shoved at Tommy's hand.

That was the wrong move, as Tommy reached and grabbed him by the collar.

"We having a problem over here?" a voice said behind me, and without turning around, I knew it was Jack.

"No problem," Garrett said, straightening his shirt as Tommy shoved him backward. "How you doin', Jack?

"All good, Garrett," Jack said. "You been hitting the whiskey pretty hard tonight. Why don't you go on home?"

"Just trying to talk to the lady." Garrett smiled. "Not looking for trouble."

"Did the lady wanna talk to you?" Jack asked.

"I think she's playing hard to get." Garrett laughed.

"Probably not," Jack said. "She's pretty outspoken. Get out of here, Garrett."

I had been watching all this with a growing admiration, but that was about to take a sharp detour south.

"She's a stuck-up tramp," Garrett hissed, his demeanor changing before my eyes. "And Jack, this is none of your damn business."

"You know, Garrett," Jack said, putting his hand on Garrett's shoulder. "You are absolutely right. It *is* none of my damn business." He turned and walked back toward his truck.

What? Is he serious? He waltzes in on a white horse like a knight in shining armor and then just leaves me here with this drunk? Of all the chickenshit moves I have ever seen, this one takes the cake! This is what is wrong with Jack Whitfield III. He's all hat and no cattle. That son of a bitch. I could claw his eyes out. And I was *going* to claw his eyes out as soon as I was done getting raped and if I didn't get murdered! Well, at least I finally knew he wasn't perfect. I was so infuriated, though, that I hardly noticed when Whiskey Breath began talking to me again.

"Whatcha say, baby?" Garrett purred. "How 'bout that ride?"

"Go to hell!" My anger at Jack fueled my rejection of Garrett. I didn't care how this drunken asshole reacted. I'd fight him myself.

I heard Ella Rae's too-loud laughter, Tommy's whoop, and then Laine's "Oh my!" about the same time I heard metal crunching and glass breaking. I looked around to see Jack's four-wheel-drive pickup on top of Garrett's Harley Davidson. After he'd driven over it the first time, he backed up and drove over it again, sufficiently crushing it.

Garrett froze and then broke into a run toward his pile of metal, screaming obscenities I had never heard before, and I was an athlete!

The girls, Tommy, and I ran over with everybody else to the mangled pile of what used to be a Harley. I was stunned. If you hadn't known that twisted mound of metal had once been a motorcycle, you could have never identified it. I slowly glanced at Jack who had gotten out of his truck and was scratching his head.

"My clutch has been sticking for a week," he said, looking at Greg Grimes who ran the auto shop in town. "I guess I need to bring her in and let you take a look."

"You son of a bitch!" Garrett yelled. "I will kill you for this!"

Jack leaned against his truck and smiled slightly. "Be careful, Garrett," he said, his voice low and even.

"Goddammit!" Garrett kicked at the remains of his bike. "You son of a bitch! Let's go, me and you! Right here!"

Jack took off his jacket and laid it on the hood of the truck. "I'm ready when you are."

Garrett's partner was dragging him back by the arm. "Hey, man," he said. "I don't think this is a good idea."

Garret made a weak effort to throw off his buddy's arm, but it was becoming pretty clear to him that his friend was right. Half the men there had already moved behind Jack and were ready to defend him, including Tommy.

"Get your ass up the road, Garrett," Jack said.

Garrett got on the back of his partner's Harley, screaming over the roar of the engine, "This ain't over, man! I'm coming for you, Jack! This ain't over!"

"It's over," Jack said, staring at him.

Garrett and his partner rode into the night with Garrett still screaming obscenities. I held my ears as the Harley roared out of sight.

Jack walked over to me. Like everyone else, I was still in awe of what had just happened. "Are you alright?"

I gazed up at him. "Umm hmm ..."

He smiled the sweetest and most tender smile that I don't think I will ever forget, leaned a little closer, and said, "Can I call you tomorrow?"

I stared at him. Had Jack Whitfield just asked if he could call me?

"Uh … well. I … uh …" I then caught a glimpse of Lexi Carter staring at us from beside Jack's truck with her hands on her hips. I may have been a lot of things, but I was no homewrecker. I looked up at him. "Aren't you and Lexi still together?"

"Not for long," he answered. "I've been waiting a long time for you to grow up. I don't think I can wait any longer."

My heart was beating wildly, and from that moment forward, it belonged to Jack Whitfield III.

I must've been smiling at the memory, because before I realized it, Jack was on the porch and standing beside the swing. "You must be thinking about football," he said.

"I didn't hear you," I confessed.

"I came in on stealth. Move over." He sat down in the swing with me.

I bit my lip. Dear Lord, he looked good all sweaty and dirty and tan. I scooted back into the seat.

"So what were you dreaming of?" he asked.

I weighed the question and decided to pull the trigger, "Actually, I was thinking about the first time you ever really talked to me." I pointed to the tree down by the driveway. "I was standing right down there."

He grinned. "I remember," he said. "You had on white shorts, an Atlanta Braves jersey, and a pair of running shoes."

That shocked me. "You remember what I was wearing?"

He shrugged. "It was a big day for me."

"Really? How so?" I was truly interested.

"It was the first time I talked to my future wife," he said. "And I knew it then."

I didn't say anything. It was pointless to let that sentence affect me, as he'd warmed up from time to time before. But the curiosity was eating me alive.

"Hmmm" was all I could manage.

He pulled me closer. "Come here, girl." He wrapped his arm around me.

Now I was thoroughly confused, but I snuggled close to him, my heart beating as wildly as it had when I was seventeen.

We sat there in silence for a little while before he spoke again. "Carrigan, I know things have been … strained between us." He paused, and I guessed he was waiting for me to speak. When I didn't, he continued. "If I asked you to do something for me, would you?"

I sighed, a torrent of emotions swirling within me. So I resorted to what had always served me best. Humor. "It doesn't involve whips, chains or leather, does it?"

He laughed. "No."

"Okay," I said. "I'm game."

He held me closer to him. "Come out to the old barn tomorrow. I've got to do a few repairs on it, and I thought if you were gonna ride Gilda, you could ride out there."

I didn't know where this was coming from or where it would end up, but I was absolutely going to the old barn tomorrow. "Okay," I answered. I had a million questions, but I said nothing. I was afraid if I asked them, the ambience would be broken and I'd never be able to get it back.

We sat in the swing in silence, his arms wrapped around me and my head on his shoulder for a long time. I still had no idea where his mood had come from, what it meant, or how to proceed from here. But I didn't want to worry about what-ifs, maybes, or anything else that would cast a shadow over this night. Tonight I wanted to be Jack's wife again. I wanted to be seventeen again and watch my knight in shining armor fight the bad guys and whisk me away on the back of a fiery steed. Being next to him felt good and right. Like I had come home.

Later that night after we'd gone to bed, Jack held me close to him all night. No sex, no talking, just lying wrapped in his arms the way we used to sleep before the indifference and distrust had somehow crept into our marriage when I wasn't looking. It was the most peaceful sleep I'd had in months. I didn't know it then, but it was also the last peaceful sleep I would have for a long, long time.

The next morning, I woke up and found a note on the pillow beside me. "Have one of the boys saddle Gilda, and meet me as soon as you can. Jack." I was ridiculously excited, like I was going on a first date. I jumped in the shower and was ready to go in thirty minutes. I grabbed an apple from the kitchen and headed out the door with Mamie begging me to let her fix my breakfast.

"I'll probably be back before lunch," I told her. "The apple will be fine."

She cackled and shook her head. "I don't think you gonna make it back for lunch, Miss Carri," she said.

I had no idea what that meant, but I flew out to the barn, had Chester saddle Gilda, and took off.

The old barn was at least a mile and a half deep into the property, and I first had to cross a soybean field, a creek, and a hayfield to get there. I enjoyed the ride; the land was well cared for. Both Jack's father and my father were all about conservation and taking care of the earth. This place was beautiful, and I loved it like it was my own.

Jack had already been working for a while when I got there. He walked outside the barn, no shirt, all tanned and muscled and sweaty. I bit my lip. There was a picnic basket under a cedar tree and a blanket next to it. Damn, I was a goner. No wonder Mamie didn't expect me for lunch; I'd be lucky to get back for Christmas. Jack took the reins from me, and I slid off Gilda into his arms. All the worries and questions that ran through my mind on a daily basis were suddenly gone. All that mattered to me was today. Maybe tomorrow I'd drown myself again in concerns about what he had or hadn't done, but today was mine. Ours.

Jack had had Mamie pack fried chicken, fruit, and a bottle of wine for lunch. We never touched it, but the wine and the blanket got a hell of a workout. It was like the man had cast a spell on me. Making love on a blanket in the July sun? Then again in the barn when a thunderstorm caught us unaware? Who was I? Last week, I had wanted to claw his eyes out of his head and today, I would've given him my soul if he'd asked for it. My husband was back. The gentle, attentive lover, whispering loving, tender words in my ear, made me feel like the only woman on earth. God, how I had missed him.

We rode back to the house slowly. I don't think either of us wanted the day to end. But it was getting dark, and there was no reception on our cell phones out in the barn. When we'd almost made it home, he stopped the horses and grabbed my hand. "Thank you, baby, for today. I know we need to talk … and we will."

I squeezed his hand. "It's okay, Jack. We'll talk."

"I love you, Carrigan. I have always loved you."

Tears sprang to my eyes. It had been so long since he'd said those words to me, and the relief was overwhelming. Suddenly, I no longer cared what he'd done or who he'd done it with. Just like that, it didn't matter to me anymore. We had both made mistakes; we'd both hurt each other. But we were still standing. We were still here, dammit. In that instant, I didn't care if everybody in Bon Dieu Falls thought I was a fool, an idiot, or any other name they wanted to call me. This was *my* Jack. How could another woman touch what was between the two of us?

I was immediately sick with regret over what I had done, for my part in the mess we had made. I was just about to tell him how sorry I was and how I loved him, when I heard a panicked voice. Ella Rae?

"Carrigan! Carrigan!"

I slid off the horse and ran toward her. Why was she here? What had happened? When I reached her, she was crying and shaking all over.

"What is it?" I said, my own voice shaking. "Ella Rae? Is it Tommy?"

She shook her head and bent to grab her knees as if to catch her breath.

Jack was beside her in an instant, holding her up and soothing her. "What is it, Rae?" he said gently. "Can you tell me?"

She grabbed his hand and finally looked up, her face wet and swollen with tears. She took a deep breath and looked into my eyes. "It's Laine," she said. "And it's bad."

Chapter 7

I knew the man was talking, I could see his lips moving. But the roaring in my ears prevented me from understanding a thing he said. I caught broken sentences once in awhile, a few words strung together, but it made no sense to me. Like a cell phone with awful reception. I stared at him, willing myself to hear him. But still, broken phrases. "Often asymptomatic ... terminal ... maybe a year ..." What the hell was he talking about? Had I lost my ability to process English? That had to be it. I stared at him again. My heart pounded in my chest, and as much as I tried, a coherent thought would not come. But mostly I was furious; it was all I could do to remain in the chair I was sitting in.

Ella Rae and I sat in the conference room on the third floor of Shreveport Medical Center with Laine's mother, Jeanette, and her brother, Michael. There was a man sitting behind a desk, a doctor, telling us that Laine had been diagnosed with stage four ovarian cancer. But surely that wasn't what he had said. I heard it, but there had to be some mistake. It wasn't true, I was sure it couldn't be true. He said the cancer had spread. He said she had a year left, maybe eighteen months with treatment. He said they could make her comfortable. I looked at Mrs. Jeanette. Stunned. I looked at Michael. Stoic. I looked at Ella Rae, who had cried so much her eyes were nearly swollen shut. She was clinging to my hand like it was a life raft. I wanted to cry too, but the tears wouldn't come. I knew they should, and I felt guilty because they wouldn't. I couldn't stay in the room much longer; it was stifling. I kept tugging at my collar in an effort to breathe.

"Do any of you have any questions for me?" the doctor said. What was his name? He had told us his name, but for the life of me, I couldn't remember it.

I looked around. Nobody said a word. They just sat there. Staring. Seriously? I had a million questions. "I'm sorry, Doctor ... I can't remember your name ..."

"Rougeau," he answered.

"Yes, Dr. Rougeau," I said, fidgeting. "I'm not sure I understand what you're saying. I mean, I get that she's ill and that it's serious, but it's treatable, right?"

The doctor cleared his throat. "As I said, I am not optimistic. But stranger things have happened."

I stared at him. "What does that even mean?"

He took a deep breath. "Ma'am, your friend is very sick. Stage four means—"

"Look, I know what stage four means. My grandfather died of lung cancer. But this is a young, healthy woman! She was riding a bicycle for miles two months ago! She cannot possibly have stage four cancer!"

He looked at me sympathetically. "I'm so sorry."

"She doesn't smoke," I said as if he hadn't spoken. "She doesn't drink more than a thimble full of fuzzy navel once a month, she takes care of herself—"

Dr. Rougeau nodded. "Sometimes, and we don't always know why, people get sick. I wish I had an explanation to give you. I just don't. We'll make her as comfortable as we can."

White-hot anger flew all over my body like I had been dipped in a vat of boiling tar. "That's it? Are you kidding me? You can make her *comfortable*? This is bullshit!" I grabbed Ella Rae's hand.

"Carrigan!," Ella Rae scolded me. "Please don't."

I heard Mrs. Jeanette apologize to Dr. Rougeau, explaining to him that Laine and I were very close and that I was very headstrong.

"Come *on*, Ella Rae," I said, pulling her from the room. I couldn't stay in there another second. It had become impossible to breathe and even more impossible to listen to that conversation. I hated the doctor for talking, and I hated everybody else for staying silent. I dragged Ella Rae down the hall so fast that we were almost jogging.

"Carri, please!" she said finally, stumbling to keep up. "Stop! Please!"

"What?" I nearly shouted at her but stopped.

"What are we gonna do?" she asked, tears spilling down her cheeks.

It hurt me to look at her. I closed my eyes and clenched my jaws together so tight that they popped. I knew I should hug and comfort her, but I couldn't. In my mind, if I acknowledged her pain, this whole nightmare would become real. I shoved her into the ladies room. "Straighten your face up," I snapped. "I don't want her to see you like this. And hurry."

I stood in the hall waiting for her and forced myself to take deep breaths. I knew I had been close to hyperventilating in that conference room, and I wasn't sure it had passed now. I couldn't pull that mess in front of Laine. I grit my teeth. If I was going to have to be the strength of this little group, so be it. If everyone else was willing to give up on Laine, that was their business. But I wasn't going to. I wasn't going to let Ella Rae give up, and I damn sure wasn't letting Laine give up on herself.

Ella Rae stepped out of the bathroom but began to cry again as soon as she looked at me. "I can't do this, Carrigan," she said.

"Yes, you can!" I told her. "You have to." I pointed down the hall toward the conference room we'd just left. "They've already buried her! You hear me?" I felt my own voice break slightly with the taste of those words. "But she's not gonna die! She just isn't! Now come on!"

Laine was asleep when we walked into her room, the remaining effects of a sedative still hanging on. A round of tests that morning had prevented us from seeing her until then. Ella Rae sat on a chair beside the bed and cried softly. There was no sense in telling her to stop; she couldn't and I knew that.

I was actually shocked when I looked at my sick and suffering friend so frail and fragile. How could Ella Rae and I have missed this? She was white as the sheet she was lying on. The dark circles under her eyes were even more pronounced because her face was so thin. I had seen her only three weeks ago. How could this have happened already? Somewhere in the back of my mind, I remembered Charlotte saying that Laine looked tired at the crawfish boil back in May, and my mother had mentioned it to me at church a couple of weeks later. Laine had even complained about being tired a time or two. Why hadn't I seen this? Was I so wrapped up in my own petty shit that I allowed a third of my lifetime trio to wither away in front of my eyes? Was I so shallow and superficial, so caught up in myself, that I couldn't see that she obviously needed help? I had dragged her all over the place when she wanted to stay home. I kept her out half the night when she didn't want to stay out. I worried the hell out of her all the time with my marriage, my affairs, and my preposterous, insane, and self-created drama. How could I not have seen this? Everything was a joke to Ella Rae and I. Everything we did was for entertainment purposes only. But not Laine. She took everything seriously—her job, the kids she taught, everything. She even took my marriage more seriously than I did.

I swallowed the bile rising in my throat. My self-loathing was palpable. I couldn't stand my own skin and wanted to claw at the thoughts inside my head.

Laine began to move her legs and, after a few moments, opened her eyes. She looked at me and then at Ella Rae, smiled slightly, and said, "I'm so sorry."

Ella Rae crumbled and laid her head on Laine's chest. They both began to sob. I was frozen, unable to react verbally or physically. It was one of the truest moments of my life. I wanted to sob along with them; the tears in my throat were as thick as the July humidity. But they wouldn't come. That in itself was anguish I couldn't describe or ignore. Surely there was something else when tears weren't enough, some other outlet for emotions I had never felt. I felt numb and inadequate. I couldn't talk or move. I just stared at them, crying quietly now and clinging to each other. I only finally moved because Laine reached out her hand to me. I walked over, sat on the side of the bed, and finally found my voice. But even it sounded strange.

"It's gonna be okay," I said.

"Of course it is," Laine agreed, but the second our eyes met, I knew neither of us believed it.

She gently pushed Ella Rae away from her. "You got my gown soaking wet, Rae."

Ella Rae was mortified. "Laine! I'm so sorry!"

Laine shook her head. "I was joking ..."

Ella Rae and I looked at her. Neither of us laughed.

"Come on," she said, sitting up in the bed. "I know this is bad. But, please, don't either of you get all weird on me."

I looked at Ella Rae, who was looking at her hands.

"Please!" Laine said more forcefully this time. "I can take it from anybody but the two of you!"

"Okay," Ella Rae and I said in unison.

"Look," Laine said. "I know this is ... shocking for you both, but I've had some time to digest it." She folded her hands in her lap and looked back and forth from Ella Rae to me. "And I need to say something to you both. Today. Right now, while it's just us. There are some things I need you to do for me, okay?"

"Okay," I said, now terribly anxious. "But look, we'll do *anything* you want us to do, but this isn't ... you know ... nobody's giving up here ... it's gonna be okay ..."

Laine smiled a little and grabbed my hand. "Just listen to me, okay?"

I sighed and nodded.

She took a deep breath. "First of all, again—never turn weird on me, okay? I'm still Laine. I'm just ... sick."

Ella Rae and I nodded.

Laine continued. "I need to know the two of you will always, always tell me the truth no matter how bad it is. I'm not sure Mother and Michael will. They want to protect me. And I know y'all do too, but promise me."

We nodded.

"And one more thing," she said, her lips trembling slightly. "I need you to both stay with me, no matter how hard it gets. 'Kay? Can you do that for me?" A tear spilled over her cheek and fell on my hand. Ella Rae began crying again, and I felt like I had been punched in the gut.

"Of course." I choked the words out.

Laine gathered her composure and cleared her throat. "I ... understand what the prognosis is. I understand the cancer is in stage four, and it is a rapidly growing type." She paused and looked at me. "I know you won't like what I'm about to say, but this is my decision, and I've made it. I have chosen not to take chemo. I don't want them injecting me with poison that won't prolong my life by much but will only make me sick for the remainder of it."

I found my voice then. "Are you crazy?" I snatched my hand from hers and stood up. "Of course you're taking chemo!"

She held up her hand. "It's not negotiable, Carrigan. And it's not your decision."

I sucked in my breath to speak again, but Laine shook her head. "Don't. Please."

I decided to let it go for the moment, but not for long. If this cancer was as aggressive as Dr. Rougeau said it was, there was no time to waste. I would somehow convince her to take the chemo. I had to.

"I am sorry for putting you both through this."

I shook my head. "Don't say that."

Ella Rae couldn't respond at all.

Laine smiled. "I'm glad y'all are here. Makes it more bearable." She closed her eyes. "I can't shake this sleeping pill. I'm gonna catch another nap, I think. You'll be here when I wake up?"

"Where else would we be?" I said.

Ella Rae held Laine's hand, and after awhile, they were both asleep. I sat in the windowsill and watched them both for a very long time. I finally looked out the window across the courtyard to the other wing. I wondered whose lives had just changed on the other side. Who'd just had the rug pulled out from under them over there? What doctor had just said, in a matter-of-fact voice, to some other unsuspecting group of loved ones that death was on the horizon, and that they'd better get used to it because they damn sure couldn't stop it? I had lost loved ones in my life—my grandparents, uncles, and aunts—and I had grieved them after they passed. But the young buried the old, that was just the way the world was supposed to work. This was Laine! A healthy, vibrant, twenty-eight-year-old woman! Nobody had ovarian cancer at twenty-eight! It was absurd! It had to be some kind of mistake. It just *had* to be.

I was mad. No, I was worse than mad, I was furious. I knew it was the reason I couldn't cry. I was mad at the doctor. How dare he speak to me like I was a child? "We'll make her comfortable? Sometimes these things just happen?" That wasn't good enough. He needed to stay out of my sight. I was mad at Laine for refusing chemo. Why on earth would she say that? Of course she was going to take chemo, if I had to administer it myself! I was mad at Ella Rae and myself for letting our friend waste away before our very eyes. The guilt I felt was like an albatross around my neck, a heavy burden that I didn't foresee lifting anytime soon. And I hoped everyone involved had the good sense not to speak to me about God. I was mad at Him most of all.

I felt a hand on my shoulder and jumped.

"Hey, baby," Jack said, kissing my forehead.

I was so glad to see him I could have crawled inside his shirt. "What are you doing here? Who's at the farm?"

"Some things are more important," he said and squeezed my hand. He looked over at Laine, still asleep and lightly snoring. "How is she?"

I didn't answer. His unexpected presence was such a relief, the tears I couldn't cry earlier were threatening now. But I couldn't cry in here, not in front Laine or even Ella Rae. Somebody had to be strong, I reminded myself. I couldn't afford the luxury of falling apart, although the temptation was gathering momentum at the speed of light.

"It's okay," he said and pulled me closer. "You don't have to answer."

I pulled away from him and faced the window again. He'd make me soft, and I couldn't afford to be soft right now. I bit my lip so hard I thought it would bleed, but I gathered my composure and said, "It's fine. I'm good. I am."

He didn't respond. I'm sure he knew what I said was complete and total bullshit but at least he didn't call me on it. "I know you'll be here with her until she goes home, so I have checked into the Hilton down the street."

I turned around then and put my hands on his arms. His daddy would have a stroke if he knew Jack was going to be gone from the farm that long. "Jack, you can't," I said. "You need to be at the farm. We'll be … okay here," I lied. I didn't know what this journey would bring. Or how long we'd be on it. The truth was I hated hospitals, but the only thing that horrified me more was leaving Laine in one.

"Carrigan, I'll be down the street until we all go home. I know what you're thinking, but Daddy would endorse this. I know this is hard for you. It is for me too." He looked at Laine. "She is … special. I'm staying."

I swallowed the lump in my throat and hugged him as tightly as I could. He loved Laine, so of course this was difficult for him. He was such a good man. Another wave of guilt washed over me of a different variety this time. How had I ever questioned who he was? Even if he'd made mistakes, so had I. But he'd always been there for me when the rubber met the road. Even at the lowest point in our lives, he'd always had my back. I shoved it from my mind. This was no time to, yet again, wallow in my disorder. I closed my eyes and lingered in his embrace.

"Cut that mess out," I heard Laine say softly, but I could hear the smile in her voice.

I smiled back at her.

Jack walked over to the bed and took her hand. "What do you need?" he asked. Straightforward, no-nonsense Jack. Always cut to the chase.

Laine shook her head and pondered for a moment. "I think I just need the people who love me to love me indeed."

"Done." He kissed her hand, held it against his face a moment, and then abruptly left the room.

The gesture melted my heart. Once again, I swallowed the ever-present lump in my throat.

"What did I just witness when I woke up?" Laine asked as the door closed, her eyes twinkling.

I smiled. "Hell freezing over?"

"Start from the beginning," she said.

Just then, Mrs. Jeanette and Michael walked in, ending our conversation.

Ella Rae stood up, and Laine's mother took her chair beside the bed. Michael stood behind her. These were two of the finest people I knew. Mrs. Jeanette had taught school for over thirty years and had just recently retired. It was easy to see where Laine's dedication to the profession and her love for the job had come from. Mrs. Jeannette had received numerous awards over the years for her performance as a teacher. I think she would've taught forever, but her health wasn't up to par. She'd struggled with rheumatoid arthritis for years, and it had recently become quite a battle. In fact, Laine had toyed with the idea of moving in with her to help her with day-to-day needs, but Mrs. Jeanette had nixed the idea. Independence was very important to her. Laine's father had died suddenly of a heart attack several years before when Laine was still in college. Laine had wanted to move home then too, but Mrs. Jeanette wouldn't hear of it. Michael lived in Shreveport, but he was married with four kids, and the twins were still in diapers. I wondered what would happen now.

Jack walked back into the room after leaving to gather his composure. He shook hands with Michael and hugged Mrs. Jeannette, asking her if he could see her in the hall. She took his hand, and he led her out.

Laine looked at me inquisitively. I shrugged.

"Carrigan," Michael said. "It's been ages since I have seen you. You look well."

"Thank you," I said. "So do you. How is Belinda and all twelve of your kids?"

He smiled. "It seems like twelve at bedtime, I assure you. But they're all doing fine."

Laine smiled. "They call me about once a week, but they all talk at one time, and I never understand a word they say."

"I haven't understood a single sentence uttered in that house for years," Michael said, and we all laughed.

"Wait'll they become teenagers," Laine said. "Good luck with that."

And uncomfortable silence followed, each of us thinking of the future and what it might hold. The subject quickly turned to the weather, the humidity, and lack of rain. Why is it, in Louisiana anyway, when a conversation becomes strained or lags the chatter turns to weather? Even in the closest circles.

Mrs. Jeanette entered the room again, clinging to Jack's hand. I could tell that she had been crying. She thanked him before she sat back down beside Laine. I had no idea what their conversation had been about, but she looked grateful and relieved.

I had been yearning to ask a question but wanted to wait until Mrs. Jeanette and Michael were both in the room. Now I had my opportunity.

I sat down on the edge of Laine's bed. "Laine, why don't we get another opinion? You know, just to be sure. I mean, doctors make mistakes all the time. They're as human as we are. This … just can't be right." Just the thought of a second opinion had given me hope. Actually, it had felt like manna pouring from heaven, giving me some sliver of control in an out-of-control situation. Of course we needed a second opinion! You didn't just get news like this and swallow it without a fight! The only thing Dr. Rougeau had left me with was despair and terror. The thought of a second opinion gave me confidence.

Laine didn't answer and began smoothing the sheets on the bed with her hands. She looked at her mother and then at Michael, who both looked at the floor.

I looked between them, waiting for somebody to answer. Nobody did. "What is it?" I asked finally. "Tell me!"

Laine took my hand in hers. "I need you to listen to me, Carrigan. You and Ella Rae both. *Really* listen, because you never do. And don't say anything till I'm done, you hear me?"

I frowned but nodded. Ella Rae nodded as well.

Laine took a deep breath, looked at Ella Rae, who had never in her life been this silent, and then looked back at me. "I have known I was sick for a while—"

"What do you mean you've known—"

Laine threw her hand up. "*Listen* to me!"

I nodded, but a thousand questions ran through my mind.

"Of course, I would've never guessed this, but later ... I thought, maybe. But that doesn't matter. This is where we are. Anyway, I already have gotten a second opinion, and a third. I don't want another one." She paused. "This is what I've been given, and this is what we'll deal with."

The room was still, save for Ella Rae's quiet weeping.

I looked from one ashen face to another and could actually feel the explosion rising inside me. *"What??"* I shouted the question and had no reservations about it. What kind of bullshit was this? Was she kidding me?

Laine sighed. "Carrigan, I knew you weren't gonna like the answer, but I need you to accept this. You ... you have to help me accept this."

Accept this?? Was she out of her mind? I wanted to punch her in the mouth. I know how that sounds, but it was the truth.

"Are you crazy?" I asked, sure they'd slipped her some sort of mind-altering drug. "Are you just gonna ... quit? And what do you mean, you have gotten three opinions? How long have you been sick? Why didn't you tell us? Who else knew? Why didn't you say anything?" I looked at Ella Rae, hoping for someone to take my anger out on. "Ella Rae, you better hope you didn't know anything about this!"

Ella Rae, still crying, finally spoke. "I didn't. I swear."

"And where did the other two opinions come from?" I demanded. "Jekyll and Hyde? Rougeau's partners? This is bullshit, Laine."

Mrs. Jeannette, ever the lady, began to look really uncomfortable, but I didn't care. I needed her to back me up. I needed *anybody* to back me up, but they all sat like statues, watching me.

"He's a good doctor, Carrigan," Laine said. "I trust him."

My mind began grasping for something that could make a difference, change the outcome, and give me just one more glimmer of optimism. I finally seized a thought through the chaos in my mind. Ah, ammunition. "Okay, okay, take the treatment! Just take the treatment! They don't know if it'll fix you or not. But miracles happen every day! So just take the treatment!"

Laine looked up at me, her eyes pleading. "Carrigan, please ..."

I saw the tears in her eyes and knew I should shut up. I *knew* I should. But I couldn't, and I didn't. "Laine! You can't just *quit*! You have to fight! You can do this; I know you can! Ella Rae and I will help you, I swear! But you have to fight!"

"Carrigan," Mrs. Jeanette said. "We all know you love her and that you're only trying to help, but this isn't helping. You need to—"

I was furious now, furious and frustrated and helpless—the worst combination of emotions imaginable for me. They made me unpredictable, irrational, and sometimes hateful.

"I need to what?" I shouted. "Dig her grave? Is that what y'all want? We could save all this shit!" I gestured wildly at the surroundings. "Let's just call the funeral home!"

"Carrigan!" Ella Rae said, horrified at my outburst. "Stop it!"

"Why?" I barked back. "I just said what everybody else is thinking, didn't I?" I looked at Laine. "So fine! If you wanna die, get after it! We're all here, and there's no time like the present. I'm ready! Do it! Do it, I *dare* you!" The tears that had threatened all day had finally started to spill, and my words were coming out in a torrent of sobs. I was powerless to stop them, even though I knew they were hateful, mean, and, on some level, cruel. But I wanted Laine to be mad at me. I wanted her to get her spirit back. I wanted her to fight! I didn't care if she never spoke to me again as long as she stayed alive.

You could've heard a pin drop in that room, but only briefly. Jack was at my side in an instant. "Come on, baby. Let's go outside."

"Let her talk, Jack," Laine said, sympathetically. "I know what she's doing. She needs to get it out."

Who else knew me like that? Who else knew it was either say it or explode? Even if it hurt the very person encouraging the words? Laine's permission broke my heart, and my anger gave way to panic. My heart pounded, and my hands were shaking. "Please, Laine," I said, softer now. I would've gotten on my knees if I thought it would have helped. "*Please* take the chemo."

She shook her head gently. "I love you, Carrigan," she whispered, "but it won't help me. I don't want to be sicker than I have to be. I'm sorry … but the answer is no."

I ran blindly out of the room, bumping into Michael and almost turning over a metal cart in the hallway. I ran down the hall, past the elevators, and down the stairs until I reached the ground floor. I ran until I found the garden I had stared down at from Laine's room. And then I cried. I cried like I hadn't cried since I was a child. Deep, mournful sobs that racked my body and came from the pit of my soul. I cried until I fell on my knees in front of the yellow roses whose beauty belied the hopelessness I felt. I was dimly aware of Jack's hands holding my hair back while I gagged and tried to catch my breath. He whispered soothing, comforting words in my ear, but they barely registered. The only voice I heard was the one in my head telling me that Laine was going to die.

Much later, I sat still on the cold stone bench in that same garden with my head on Jack's shoulder, my eyes swollen from crying. The sun was setting in the western sky, birds were singing, and people walked by laughing, going on with their lives. All these things dismayed me. Didn't they know Laine was dying? How the hell could life just go on? I knew, of course, that it wasn't their fault, but I hated them all just the same. This had blindsided me. It was like a sucker punch. It had happened to me on the softball field once years before. I was standing on second base, not paying attention, and got hit in the head by a line drive I didn't see coming. Next thing I knew, I woke up in the hospital. This was the exact same feeling. Once again, I wasn't paying attention, got hit by a line drive, and woke up in the hospital. Only this time it had happened to my heart.

Chapter 8

"*I* had forgotten how pretty this place is." Laine was sitting in the big wicker swing on the porch at Whitfield Farms. "So many times when I'm here, it's for a party or a get-together, and there are people everywhere. But when it's still like this … it's gorgeous."

I smiled. She was right. This was a beautiful place. Huge oak trees well over a hundred years old dotted the landscape in every direction. Mrs. Diane was a master gardener, and her rose garden was the envy of every lady in Bon Dieu Falls. The yard and flowerbeds were pristine and beautiful, not because hired hands kept them that way, but because she did. Lush green fields were just beyond the wood fence where cattle and horses grazed. Soon the leaves would be turning and the mums would be blooming. Time seemed to fly by these days. None of us had ever been so acutely aware of that before.

Two months had passed since that awful day in the hospital. We'd settled in nicely here at Jack's parents' home. Laine had stayed in the hospital for exactly a week and had been there three days before Ella Rae or I even knew it. She'd taken a severe scolding from both of us over that. They'd run all the tests she would allow, cauterized the original tumor in her ovaries to keep it from bleeding, and given her pain medication, although she still insisted she didn't need it. I wasn't sure if that were the truth or not, but if it wasn't, she hid it well.

Jack had talked with Mrs. Jeanette the day I had my meltdown in Laine's hospital room. She'd agreed to encourage Laine to stay here at the farm with us during her illness. Mrs. Jeanette was unable to care for her the way she would need to, and Jack convinced her it was a win-win for everyone involved. He'd asked her to move in as well, but she declined. But she came every day, and we'd even convinced her to spend a night here and there. But she couldn't bring herself to impose upon us like that, she said. We had tried in vain to assure her there would be no imposition. The plantation-style house was huge with plenty of room and wraparound porches, balconies, and all those things you see in a southern novel. It had been in the Whitfield family for generations. Mr. Jack and Mrs. Diane were wholeheartedly in agreement with the arrangement. Anybody would be hard-pressed to find two finer people than my father- and mother-in-law. In my mind, my love for them was second only to my love for my own parents. They had a house full of people now, and they loved it.

Jack had hired a registered nurse to be there around the clock, something else Laine insisted she didn't need. But she sure made the rest of us feel better. Her name was Debra Pierson and came highly recommended from a family Mr. Jack knew who had retained her services during a similar situation. Debra was in her late forties, had never been married, and had no children. She was friendly and cordial, but she was no-nonsense. She kept a close eye on Laine and ate meals with us, but after she was done with both, she disappeared into her room. I'm not sure she understood the whole living arrangement we had going on at Whitfield Farms, but at least she'd had the good sense not to question it.

Mamie, however, was having a ball. She loved to "cook large" as she put it. Mamie was Webster's definition of nurturer. She asked Laine every morning what she wanted for supper and every night, it seemed. Laine ate like a bird, but I didn't think that was a cancer thing. At least, I told myself it wasn't. She'd never had a huge appetite, I reasoned. But I watched her like a hawk just the same. I made sure her favorite things were always in the house—orange Popsicles and saltwater taffy. She wasn't gaining weight, but at least she hadn't lost any either. I, on the other hand, had picked up seven unwanted pounds, and Ella Rae had gained five. The fried chicken in this house should have been on the front of every cookbook that came out of Southern United States. I don't know what made it so different, but I was sure glad Laine asked for it on a regular basis. I told her all the time that if Bethany Wilkes took Jack away from me, it was going to be her fault. But she scoffed at that, assuring me that Jack wouldn't leave me for a supermodel. I finally became convinced that she was right.

Jack had asked my mother to pack my things while Laine was still in the hospital, as I had not been back to my house since we arrived here. In fact, I don't think I had left the property. Ella Rae was with us too. Tommy was in Texas working, so I didn't have to ask her twice. Most of our days were spent on one of the porches at the farm or riding around the place on an ATV. There was a time when that would've sounded so boring to me; I would've compared it to watching paint dry. But time had become more precious to all of us than any other thing. We squeezed every second from every day and hated to go to bed at night.

One day, we were sitting on the front porch, sipping lemonade and watching Jack and the hands repair the roof on the stables.

"Don't you get nervous when he's walking around on the roof?" Ella Rae asked, hiding her eyes with her hands. "I'm nervous for you."

I laughed. "Jack is like a cat." I watched him, admiring his tanned chest that glistened in the sun. I bit my bottom lip.

Laine cackled. "I never thought I'd see it, but you are lusting after your husband!"

I made a face. "Lusting? Where are we, in the fifties? I was merely appreciating my choice of mates."

"It sure sounded like you were appreciating him last night," Ella Rae chimed in.

"Seriously!" Laine agreed.

"What?" I said, a little embarrassed by the memory. We had been making up for lost time, but I hadn't realized everybody in the house knew it.

They both began laughing, and I was mortified. I'd talk about anything with these women, but I drew the line at sex. Even in my extracurricular moments, they may have known it happened, but they didn't know details. My contention had always been if we weren't having sex, we weren't going to talk about sex. It was my version of being a lady—although that was one thing I'd never been accused of.

"Do you think Mr. Jack and Mrs. Diane heard us too?" I asked, my face.

"How could they help it?" Ella Rae said. "It sounded like y'all were swinging on the chandeliers!"

"Oh my God," I groaned and slid down into the wicker swing.

"Did I hear you praying last night too?" Laine asked. "Cause somebody kept saying 'oh God, oh God' over and over again."

They rolled all over themselves, laughing, and I took a swing at Ella Rae. "Y'all are both lying!" I said, realizing I had waltzed into that one. "Nobody hollered 'oh God'!" Still, I was horrified because I had just given myself away.

Laine recovered and patted my hand. "It's okay, Carri. You're married to him, so you get to do anything you want to do with him."

"Y'all know payback is hell, don't you?" I said.

"Ain't nobody worried with you," Ella Rae said, rolling her eyes.

I smiled and looked back at Jack driving nails into the roof of the stable. The past two months had done wonders for our relationship. For two people who'd been headed to divorce court six months ago, this turnaround had been nothing short of miraculous. It started the day of the picnic, that perfect day that had turned into a perfect nightmare when Ella Rae had shown up at dusk. Jack had changed after that or, as Laine pointed out later, maybe I had. Regardless, whatever happened, Jack and I had somehow gotten back to the point of our beginning. All the worries and insecurities that had plagued me for two years were suddenly and implausibly gone. The things that had mattered most didn't matter at all anymore. I didn't care what he'd done, who he'd done it with, or why it had happened. It was as if I couldn't remember the anxiety I had felt, the all-consuming need to get back at him, the insanity that went with all the emotions that surrounded that time.

But what I did remember with white-hot shame were the two

Adonis's I had used to exact revenge. I was nearly devoured with the need to confess it to Jack. I had never felt any guilt about it until now, at least not in reference to Jack. "He had done it first" was always my contention. But now I wanted to bare my soul, make a clean slate. But Ella Rae had advised against it. In fact, she railed against it. She ranted and raved and cited a hundred different reasons why it was the "stupidest idea you've ever had, and face it, you've had a few." No argument there, but still, I wasn't convinced. I wanted some sort of penance, I guess. Either that or I wanted Jack to know that although they had touched my body, they had never touched my heart.

In the end, it was Laine who convinced me that it wasn't a good idea. "I understand the need," she had said, "and maybe it'll purge your guilt. But it'll only hurt Jack. You say it doesn't matter to you anymore what he did or didn't do. What makes you think it matters to him? It was six months ago, Carrigan. Let it go." That had clicked for me. What good would it really do? She had advised me to go to God with my guilt, and He would show me how to release it. I agreed, but I wasn't interested in talking to God. About anything. Laine trusted Him completely, without reservation, but He was the maestro of her circumstances, wasn't He? No, I had nothing to say to God.

"What's on the menu tonight, Laine?" Ella Rae asked.

"It's a surprise," she answered.

"I hope it's not fried chicken again," I said patting my backside. "My wardrobe can't afford it."

Ella Rae pinched a make-believe roll on her stomach. "Mine either!"

Later that night, we all sat around the dining room table while Mamie put the finishing touches on supper.

"I'm just saying," Laine explained, "in most circles, this meal is considered dinner."

"The hell you say," Tommy frowned. "What do they call dinner?"

"Lunch," Laine smiled.

"I don't understand folks sometimes." Tommy shook his head.

Tommy had gotten a week off and had driven out to the farm to surprise Ella Rae. She had squealed with delight when she saw him. I felt like doing that when Jack was on the roof today. Maybe my marriage wasn't so unlike Ella Rae and Tommy's after all. Well, except for the little detour we'd taken.

I was so hungry I could have eaten the plates off the table, but Mamie was taking her own sweet time tonight. She didn't allow anyone in the kitchen for supper preparation. Any of us could hang around for breakfast or lunch, but when it came to supper, she fancied herself as Picasso with a spatula. I was very excited when the French doors that led to the kitchen swung open, and Mamie appeared with a platter. I just knew it was fried chicken, and my mouth was already watering. But when she sat the platter down, it was full of sunny-side up eggs. Mrs. Diane followed with platters of bacon, sausage, and biscuits. I was immediately disappointed, but this was Laine's favorite meal, right after fried chicken. I don't know why she would've said it was a surprise.

When the platter came my way, Jack tipped the platter and slid two of the eggs onto my plate. I don't think I have ever been that queasy in my life. And then it hit me like a ton of bricks. I bolted from my chair and into the nearest bathroom just beyond the kitchen. Jack was close on my heels.

"Are you alright?" he asked, kneeling down beside me.

"Ugh ..." I answered. "Those eggs. Did you see how they were shaking?"

He chuckled. "I didn't notice a shake."

"Hand me a washcloth, will you?" I asked.

He wet the cloth and gave it to me. The cool, wet cloth did the trick, and the nausea passed as quickly as it had appeared. "That was weird," I said and shook my head.

"When was your last period?" Ella Rae asked from the bathroom door.

"What? How long have you been standing there?"

"Long enough to realize what you idiots can't figure out." Ella Rae smiled. "When was your last period?"

I looked up at Jack, who was staring down at me. The look on his face matched mine—pure and absolute astonishment.

"Uhhh … I think probably … let's see."

"These are not difficult questions, Carri," Ella Rae said.

"Really!" Laine chimed in.

"Who else is out there?" I asked.

"Just us," Ella Rae said. "Now think! Look, Laine. Her boobies are huge!"

"What?" I looked down at my chest. Damn! Where'd those come from?

I looked at Jack again who was now wearing a little lopsided grin. "Well?" he asked softly.

I thought back. I knew it had been after the crawfish boil and then before Laine had been in the hospital, so that meant … Holy shit. I looked at Jack again and whispered, "June." And this was the first week of September.

Ella Rae let out a huge "Woohoo!" that brought the rest of the house running. Picture this. I'm sitting on the floor of the bathroom, hands still hugging the toilet seat. Jack is still sitting on the edge of the tub beside me. Ella Rae is doing what later becomes known as the "baby dance," and Laine is pumping her fist in the air like the Tigers just converted a fourth and five, not that she would have known what that meant. Then my mother- and father-in-law, Laine's mother, Tommy, and Mamie all joined in.

That night, we did what Louisiana folks do best. We had a party at the drop of a hat. Laine called my mother, who called my sister, who called a few of our friends, and we celebrated Baby Whitfield. Or I should say *they* celebrated Baby Whitfield. Jack and I mostly stood around in shock. Although he was certainly in better shape than I was. At least he was talking.

Looking back, I'm sure I was in some mild form of shock. In one of those weird cocoons when you're so freaked out from a bolt out of the blue, you feel like you've had a little of Cousin Frankie's weed. I didn't share that feeling, of course, but if someone had asked me to compare it to something, that's the first thing I would've thought of. I grasped for every straw I could think of. Maybe it was something else, right? I'd certainly been under a lot of stress lately. Couldn't that cause your little friend not to show up? I mean, I couldn't be pregnant! I could barely take care of myself!

I went over and over the last couple of months in my mind. I had gotten off my pills in May and was going to take the birth control shots. I was in no hurry to get back to Shreveport to my gynecologist, for there was no point. I hadn't seen Adonis in months, and Jack and I were barely speaking. Then we'd gone to stay at the farm when Mrs. Diane and Mr. Jack left on their cruise. Then we had that picnic … quite a picnic, apparently. Then when Laine got sick, I just never thought about it again.

Ella Rae and Tommy had gone into town to buy a home pregnancy test, but there was no need to even take it. I knew it was true. I started remembering little things I passed off the last few weeks as insignificant. After all, there were things of a much greater concern going on here without whining about a backache or the horrible smell of coffee in the mornings or the constant and irrational craving for orange Popsicles. It was a unique time for all of us, and I assumed we were all in some way adjusting to the new normal. Besides, I had always hated the smell of coffee. It had just never made me want to projectile vomit until lately. So I had, in layman's terms, blown it off.

I stepped out onto the patio and quietly closed the door behind me. I needed to be alone for a few minutes and let this information sink in. I also needed to decide how I really felt about this. That may sound like a horrible thing to say, but the truth was, this couldn't have happened at a worse time. I didn't want to terminate it. I knew that. I *wanted* Jack's baby. I just didn't know I did until now, but I did. Still, I didn't want any attention taken away from Laine. I could be pregnant anytime. She was only going to … die … once. That thought punched me in the gut like it always did.

I sat down on the metal patio bench and looked out into the field. The next few months should be about Laine and only Laine. She deserved that. It's why she was here. And here I was, stealing the show again, like I always did. No matter what I was doing, Laine had always been in the background either cheering me on or screaming at the top of her lungs for me to stop. It seemed unfair that I couldn't give her center stage even when she was about to exit the show.

"Hey," Laine said.

I looked up and saw her standing in the patio door. "Hey," I said.

She walked over and sat down beside me. "Are you okay?"

I didn't answer. The tears that I had found so hard to come by most of my life now flowed like a faucet at least once a day, even though I hid to shed them. But there was no hiding them tonight.

"Carri, what's the matter?" I could hear the concern in her voice. "You are happy about this, aren't you? The baby, I mean?"

I nodded. "Of course I am." I started to blubber a little. "It's just ..."

"What?" she asked.

I shook my head again but didn't answer. How could I tell her that I wanted her to star in her own death show and that my being pregnant would steal her thunder? I couldn't. So I just cried instead.

She grabbed my hand. "Carrigan! This baby ... it *is* Jack's, isn't it?"

Jolted back to reality, I snatched my hand from hers and stared at her. "Are you shitting me? Of course it's Jack's baby, you dipshit!"

She laughed and grabbed my hand again. "Like that was a ridiculous question?"

"I may be stupid, but I ain't *that* stupid!"

She laughed again. "Okay, my bad. I was just making sure. But if it isn't that, what is it? Tell me."

"Laine, I ..." I tried to make the words come out. "This is a really bad time for ... what I mean is ..."

"Ah, I see. You think this would be a crappy time for you to be pregnant while I'm ... ill."

"Yes!" I said, relieved that she'd said the words and I didn't have to.

She stood up and stared down at me, angry. "Are you out of your mind?"

I was a little shocked. "What do you mean?"

"What better time could there be?" she asked, her hands on her hips. "It's ... it's ... life restoring itself!" She gestured around us. "It happens on this farm every day with plants and animals. It's the natural order of things! It is a *blessing*, Carrigan! Trust me."

I stared at her. She had amazed me the way she'd accepted her death sentence. She spoke matter-of-factly about it and wanted everyone else to speak about it the same way. Well, I couldn't. I couldn't accept it or talk about it like it was a weather report or a football score. I wanted to, and I knew it would make the days easier, but I couldn't. And I hadn't wanted her to either, but it was already too late. It was almost like she embraced it. I hated that part of her. Hated it. But I went along with it because when I didn't, it upset her.

She knelt in front of me. "Carrigan, I couldn't be any happier than I am about this. I *love* you. I have always wanted this for you! For you and Jack. Don't you see? It gives me a reason to … hang on." Tears filled her eyes then. "This is going to be an amazing time! Please don't try to downplay it or restrain it or act like it isn't a big deal. It's a *huge* deal!"

I weighed her words and sighed. I wanted to be happy and excited and all those things I was supposed to be when you find out you're pregnant. I wanted to celebrate too. But I felt so guilty about it. Laine deserved a happily ever after, but I was the one who was getting it. How could I rejoice and mourn at the same time?

She sat down beside me and put her arm around my shoulder. "This baby is a gift for me," she said. "Don't you understand that? And I know what you're thinking." She paused. "Look at me."

I turned my face to hers.

"I *will* see this baby. I promise you I will."

I hugged her so hard I was afraid I had hurt her. "Thank you," I whispered.

Ella Rae popped her head out of the patio door and produced a pregnancy test. "Time to pee on a stick!" she announced.

Great. Just what I always wanted. Fifty people standing outside the bathroom door, waiting for me to pee.

I held my hand out to Laine to pull her from the bench. "Let's go find a potty."

She smiled. "First time I've ever heard you say those words sober."

Chapter 9

The following weeks were filled with excitement and preparation for the baby. You would've thought I was giving birth to royalty the way everybody treated me. Mamie checked every morning with Laine and me to see what we wanted to eat the rest of the day and made sure both of us cleaned our plates. But she kept eggs off my menu, as I still couldn't bear the thought of them. Luckily, I craved fresh fruit and pancakes. I was forced to sneak orange Popsicles, though, because Mamie thought I was eating too much sugar. So I made Jack buy some and put them in the freezer in the barn where they kept the animal meds. But I think he counted them as well. Mamie even had him on board with the sugar thing.

I'd been to the doctor—correction, Jack, Ella Rae, Laine, and I had been to the doctor, and my due date was April third. I looked at Laine when Dr. Davis told us the date, and she reached over and squeezed my hand. I'm sure everyone in the room understood that gesture. I was torn between wishing the days would pass quickly so the baby would get here and Laine could enjoy him or her and wishing they'd slow down so we'd have more time with Laine. It was a terrible conflict of emotions.

Mrs. Diane was the chairperson of the baby's room committee at the farm. Jack said she was a slave driver. He and Ella Rae had painted the room four different times, and each time Mrs. Diane came in and said, "Too pale" or "Too bright," and they had to start over. Every time, I asked him what color it was, and he'd shake his head and say, "Yellow."

Nobody would let Laine or me even remotely near the paint fumes, so we spent most mornings on the front porch sipping Mamie's smoothie concoctions and talking. My favorite was the coconut pineapple that tasted like a piña colada but without the rum. It was delicious.

"Laine," I said the morning before Thanksgiving, "do you remember one night years ago when we were frog hunting in the creek behind Ella Rae's house?"

She rolled her eyes. "How could I forget? I'm still carrying the scar where you tried to kill me. This coconut smoothie is my favorite," she added, taking a big gulp.

"Mine too. Listen, that knife slipped out of my hand while you were shrieking about an alligator. That whole cut thing wasn't my fault."

"Whatever," she said. "Funny, I never get injured unless you or Ella Rae are around."

"Ha, ha," I said.

"What made you think about that night?"

I slurped the rest of my drink and put the glass on the wicker table. "That was the night you told me you had a secret. Something you'd never told Ella Rae or me. I've asked you ten times a year since then to tell me, and you always said you'd tell me someday." I paused for effect and looked at her. "You think we're there yet?"

"I wondered when you were gonna bring that up." She smiled and stirred the last of her drink with her straw for a few moments. Finally, she said, "You know, I think that day has arrived."

I sat up in my chair on full alert and mindlessly rubbed my baby bump that was quickly becoming quite pronounced. "Then do tell!" I said. "And this better be good. I've waited on it for years!"

She chuckled. "I think you'll find it ... interesting."

"I'm ready!" I was truly excited to hear Laine's deep, dark secret. Of course, she was probably about to tell me she'd cheated on a test in fifth grade or stuck her tongue out at her mother when she was nine or some other offense she believed would send her to a fiery hell. Regardless, I was eager to hear the confession.

She smiled and turned in the swing to face me. She looked tired, and although I knew she'd never admit it, I knew that she was in some pain lately. I questioned Debra about it but didn't get very far. She was fiercely protective of Laine's privacy and had repeatedly told me when I asked questions that it was something I should ask Laine. I supposed that's what nurses were supposed to do, but the only response I ever got from Laine was a pat on my hand and an "I'm fine." It was extremely frustrating.

"This may shock you a little bit," Laine warned me.

I made a face. "Really? Because I am so sweet and innocent, your terrible deed, whatever it was, is gonna make me pee my pants, I'm sure."

She laughed a little bit and then took a deep breath. "Do you remember Mitch Montgomery?"

The name sounded familiar, but I couldn't place him. "Maybe," I said. "Why do I know that name?"

"He went to high school with us but only our junior and senior years."

I thought back, and then it hit me. I did remember him. "Lots of curly black hair? Tall? Quiet guy?"

"Yep," Laine confirmed. "That's him."

"What about him?"

"He was in college at ULM the same time I was," she explained. "I had seen him on campus a few times, but he'd cut his hair short, and I wasn't sure it was him, so I never spoke. Then one day, I saw him off campus at a coffee shop." She took a deep breath before continuing. "So we had dinner together that night and ... breakfast the next morning."

I stared at her. "So?"

"We had *breakfast* the next morning," she repeated.

I kept staring at her. "People eat, Laine. Was it like the best breakfast you've ever had? I mean ..." And then it dawned on me. She had *breakfast* with him the next morning! "You *slept* with Mitch Montgomery?" I hadn't meant to shout.

"Thank you," she said, looking around. "I'm quite sure the farm hands wanted to know!"

"I'm sorry, but, Laine ... I mean, you're, you never ... You're a virgin!" I finally blurted.

"No, you and Ella Rae always said I was." She smiled. "I just never confirmed or denied."

My mind was racing. The fact that Laine had sex with Mitch Montgomery wasn't a big deal to me, but the fact that she'd never told Ella Rae and me was huge. I was brimming with questions. "Why didn't you tell us? What happened? Where is he? Was it just a one-night thing or did you have a relationship with him? Tell me everything! Were you in love with him?"

"Crap, Carrigan!" She laughed. "Which question do you want me to answer first?"

"Can I tell Ella Rae?" I asked.

"Of course," she said. "But don't scream it!"

"Ella Rae!" I shouted. "Come out here! And bring a Popsicle!"

"You have always been so loud!" Laine accused. "And I think being preggers just made you worse!"

Ella Rae appeared a few moments later with a Popsicle in one hand and a paintbrush in the other. "What is it?"

"Sit down," I said. "Laine, tell her."

Laine opened her mouth, but I changed my mind and cut her off. "Let me! Let me!" I said.

She waved her hand and laughed. "Be my guest."

"Laine had sex with Mitch Montgomery." I announced smugly.

Ella Rae frowned. "Today?" she asked.

My delight in sharing the secret was immediately deflated. "Yes, Ella Rae," I said, exasperated. "While you were painting and I was in the rocking chair next to her, Mitch Montgomery drove up and they had sex in the porch swing."

Ella Rae made a face. "What are you talking about?"

Laine had started laughing wholeheartedly, and it was contagious. "Ella Rae, when I was in college at ULM, I had a ... a fling with Mitch Montgomery."

Ella Rae rolled her eyes. "Whatever. You're a virgin. And who the hell is Mitch Montgomery?"

"I am *not* a virgin!" Laine defended.

That was even funnier, and now all three of us were laughing, even though Ella Rae had no idea why.

"Okay, okay," Ella Rae finally said after we'd composed ourselves. "Somebody tell me what the hell."

Laine recounted the story while Ella Rae listened intently. When she was finished talking, Ella Rae asked the same twenty questions I did.

"I swear you two are the exact same person sometimes!" Laine said. "Okay, it happened my senior year. It lasted six months, and it was wonderful. Yes, I was in love with him, and yes, I believe he was in love with me. And I didn't tell either of you because … I knew from the beginning it wouldn't last."

We were hanging onto her every word. In some circles, a college fling confession wouldn't normally be that big a deal, but in our case, this news was enormous. How could Laine have kept this kind of secret all these years? She'd graduated from ULM eight years ago!

"How did you know it wouldn't last?" I asked. "He didn't want to move back to Bon Dieu Falls or something?"

"He wanted to move to the city and become an actor?" Ella Rae chimed in.

I shook my head at Ella Rae's question. The girl was an island.

Laine chuckled at Ella Rae, but then she got quiet again.

"What happened, Laine?" I said.

She took a deep breath. "Mitch had gotten married his freshman year at ULM. He met a girl, starting dating her, she got pregnant, and they got married."

She paused when she saw our stunned expressions. Our Laine involved with a married man? Neither of us spoke.

"They were separated," she said quickly as if she read our thoughts. "In fact, they had already filed the divorce papers before I entered the picture."

"Wow," I said. "I knew that didn't sound like anything you'd be a part of. Not that I would judge you. I mean, things happen, you know."

"For real," Ella Rae agreed.

"So why didn't it work out?" I asked.

Laine shook her head. "I knew in the end that he would choose his son over me," she said, her eyes brimming. "And I've never blamed him for that. It's what he should have done. We kept in touch for a year or so after they got back together, but I just never felt right about it. You know, a man living with his wife and child but professing his undying love to me. It just felt so … wrong. I eventually told him not to contact me anymore."

Ella Rae and I were quiet. What did you say to something like that? My heart ached for her.

"I'm so sorry, Laine," I finally said. "You deserved so much more."

She shrugged. "It's fine. Water under the bridge, and I don't regret it. Not a second of it. You both always wondered why I wouldn't date anybody over once or twice. Well, Mitch was the reason. Nobody else ever measured up, I guess. Maybe it was wrong, but I loved him."

"It wasn't wrong," Ella Rae said. "He was almost divorced. They weren't together. You didn't pull them apart."

Laine nodded. "I know."

A brief silence followed before Ella Rae asked what I'd been dying to but wasn't sure I should. "Do you want to see him again? I mean, you know, since …"

"Since I'm dying anyway, so what difference would it make now?" Laine offered.

"Ugh …" I said, hating the death reference. "I don't think that's what—"

"Oh, come on," Laine said. "Y'all promised me from the beginning we'd call a spade a spade. Don't back out on me now!"

I shook my head. "Fine. Since you're dying anyway, do you want us to find him? Tell him? Do you wanna speak to him again?"

Laine looked out across the field thoughtfully. "I admit, I have thought about it. Just to tell him good-bye, you know? And to make sure his life has been happy." She looked back at us. "But what good would it do now? It's done, and there's no changing it. Maybe it would just mess him up, and I would never do that to him."

"Piss on him!" Ella Rae said.

"Ain't that the truth!" I said. If Mitch Montgomery were in front of me right then, I'd beat him to a bloody pulp. He left her, and she was still trying to protect him? To hell with that! "What do *you* want, Laine?"

"Don't. Please, don't do that," she said. "It wasn't his fault."

Neither Ella Rae nor I commented. Laine could take up for Mitch all she wanted to, but the fact remained that he left her and she loved him. She'd been young and naïve. He was married, for Christ's sake! He had known the score. But if she wanted to defend him, I'd keep my mouth shut.

"Sorry," I muttered.

"Me too," Ella Rae said. "But I don't mean it."

Laine laughed. "I love you both for supporting me, but its okay. Really. I learned how to live with it a long time ago."

"But promise to tell us if you want to talk to him, Laine," Ella Rae said. "Really. We'll find him. Promise?"

She smiled. "I promise. And listen, now is a good time to say something to both of you too." She sat up straight and looked back and forth between us. "And just listen to me, okay? I really want to say this."

We both nodded and waited for her to continue.

"I wouldn't trade a second of this friendship, do you hear me? Not a night when either or both of you were too drunk to drive so I had to. Not being dragged out to a creek at midnight so y'all could skinny-dip. Not a time when I had to stand between you and somebody you wanted to punch, Ella Rae, and not even the night you punched me! I don't regret taking you to meet somebody you had no business meeting, Carrigan. Maybe it was wrong, but you are my friend, and I love you. I wouldn't trade a single thing about my life, and that means Mitch too. He may have been the only man I have ever loved, but the two of you were the real loves of my life. The ones I could always count on to beat up a bully in first grade or come to my rescue or watch me walk to my house in the dark or help me look for a lost dog for three days. I was never lonely, and I was never afraid I wouldn't have somebody to do something with. Some people go their entire lives without a friend like that, and I've had two. I have been so blessed. And I am blessed now. Look at all this." She gestured around her. "Who gets to go out like this? I love you both so much."

Ella Rae, of course, had begun crying after the first sentence and reached for Laine's hand. "I love you too. I wish you didn't have to go."

"Me too." Laine smiled and wiped her tears. "But I don't make the rules."

I felt the tears stinging my eyes but managed to will them not to fall. Then when Laine mentioned the Rule Maker, my hurt turned to anger right away. If I lived to be one hundred, I would never understand the logic behind Laine's illness. If God wanted me to talk to Him, He needed to answer some questions first, and so far, He'd been silent.

"Enough," Laine said. "I don't want to waste our days on tears. Let's see the baby bump today."

Glad to get off the subject, I raised my t-shirt.

Laine shook my belly slightly. "Asleep?"

"All morning," I confirmed. "Probably so he can wiggle all night."

"She," Laine corrected.

I smiled. I didn't have a feeling either way, and Jack and I had decided not to find out.

"You know that's Henry the Eighth," Ella Rae piped up. "Or Jack the fourth. Whatever." She and Jack had been convinced from the start that the baby was a boy.

Jack walked up the steps then and patted my belly. "Jackson Madison Whitfield the Fourth," he said. "What's my boy been doing today?"

Engrossed in the daily fight over the sex of my child, the Mitch Montgomery conversation was forgotten. It wasn't until later that night while I listened to Jack's even breathing in bed beside me that I slipped out of bed, sat in the window seat, and thought about it again. Laine had certainly surprised me, and my heart truly ached for her. Not just because of the circumstances but because she never shared the burden with us. Things had always been easier for me because of Ella Rae and Laine. Whether it was choosing an outfit or some problem I couldn't solve, they had always been my sounding boards and touchstones. They kept me grounded, and even when they didn't agree with me or downright told me I was an idiot, I could always take my problems to them. I couldn't imagine my life without either of them, although the day was approaching when I'd have to.

"Hey, baby," Jack said sleepily. "You okay?"

"I'm fine." I went back to bed, laid my head on his chest, and closed my eyes, but sleep didn't come for a very long time.

Chapter 10

*L*aine began hemorrhaging one evening early in December. It
came out of the blue and scared the hell out of us all. Debra had
taken over in an instant, and I developed a new respect for her. She had
us all rounded up and into Mr. Jack's SUV within five minutes to take
Laine to the hospital.

After a procedure to cauterize the tumor and a blood transfusion,
we went home three days later. Ella Rae had spent the nights at the
hospital with Laine and her mother, but Jack had insisted that he and
I stay at the Hilton. I was nearly six months into my pregnancy and
already couldn't find a comfortable position.

Laine had rallied after the transfusion and actually looked and felt
better than she had in weeks. Christmas had been a happy time at the
farm for everyone, but I couldn't seem to dredge up the spirit. I tried
not to let it permeate everything, but in my heart of hearts, I knew this
was Laine's last Christmas. I was moody and weepy most of the month
but managed to sell it as a pregnant woman's hormone wars. At least, I
sold it to everybody but Jack.

"I don't know why you think you have to be brave even when we're
alone," he told me in bed on Christmas Eve. That was all it took. I
cried myself to sleep on his shoulder and woke up Christmas morning,
determined to have a good day. And it certainly was. The house was
filled to the brim with family—Jack's, Ella Rae's, Laine's, and mine. It
had been a joyful day, full of laughter and love. Laine had given Ella Rae

and me a picture that she had enlarged and framed. It was a snapshot of the three of us sitting on the old stone bridge at Willow Creek. The bridge had long been out of use and was covered in moss and ferns. We must've been around twenty-one or twenty-two. Laine was pointing to something in the water, and Ella Rae was looking at it, smiling. I had my head thrown back, laughing. It was a beautiful, unplanned shot that somehow caught the spirit of us all. It remains to this day one of my most prized possessions.

When New Year's Eve arrived, Jack had planned a fireworks show at the farm. One of his buddies owned a demolition company, and another one owned a fireworks company. When he told me about it, I was a little apprehensive. I'd been around Sean O'Reilly, his explosives friend. He blew up a beaver dam back in the field by the old barn years ago, and I swear I felt the earth move. But Jack assured me there would be no holes in the earth this time, and that Sean had gotten much better at what he did now. As it turned out, Jack was right; the show didn't disappoint. It was spectacular.

The farm had become the gathering place for close friends and family as the months went by, and New Year's Eve brought a huge crowd. I wasn't sure why, but rubbing my belly had become like a lucky charm. I swear thirty people touched my stomach that night. It didn't bother me; I had become accustomed to it, but I don't think Jack ever really liked it. Long about ten o'clock, he came and stood behind me and laced his fingers across my stomach.

"Are you jealous?" I laughed.

"No," he replied. "I'd just rather not watch everybody in town lay their hands on you."

"So you *are* jealous," I said again, teasing.

"Probably," he admitted finally, smiling. "Anyway, problem solved."

The stroke of midnight came. Everyone toasted with champagne, but of course, I had apple juice. This pregnancy had been relatively easy, save for a few times when the nausea was unbelievable. But for a girl who used to be able to party until the wee hours, when ten p.m. came, I was ready to go to bed. So staying up until midnight had been a stretch for me. I said goodnight to the crowd and climbed the stairs to our bedroom. Jack walked up with me and asked me if I wanted him to stay.

"No, not at all." I told him. "Go mingle with the peeps. I'll be asleep as soon as my head hits the pillow."

He nuzzled my neck. "What if I want to love on my wife when I come to bed?" he asked.

"You do whatever you gotta do, buddy," I said, putting my hands on either side of his face. "Just don't wake me up."

"Damn," he winced and held his chest. "You got me." He popped me on the backside with his palm and slipped out the door before the pillow I threw hit him.

I had just turned off the light when the bedroom door opened again. Without turning over, I said, "Give it up, Jack Whitfield. No sex tonight."

"Come on," Laine giggled. "Just one time."

I flipped on the light to find Laine and Ella Rae standing in my bedroom, each covered in confetti and streamers and holding a wine bottle. "What the hell are y'all doing?" I asked.

"What the hell are *you* doing?" Laine asked, giggling.

"Ella Rae! Did you let her get drunk? You know she's not supposed to drink while she's taking pain pills!" I sat up in bed and threw the covers off.

"Will you chill the hell out?" Ella Rae said. "She's only had like, I don't know, one bottle of wine." Ella Rae looked at her own bottle. "And I've only had, like, three."

"A whole bottle?" I gasped. "She can't drink a shot glass of alcohol, Rae, you know that! Sit down, Laine. Are you okay?"

She plopped down on the overstuffed chair and rolled her eyes. "You need to get over yourself, missy. And by the way, I did have my medication, and I did wash it down with wine, and it was goooooood!"

I laughed in spite of myself, and Ella Rae cackled.

"Here's what," Ella Rae said as she jumped into my bed and stuffed the pillows behind her. "Laine got a little drunk—"

"I said not to say drunk!" Laine scolded her.

"I mean tipsy!" Ella Rae corrected herself. "Laine got a little tipsy so she could explain death to us."

"What??" I asked.

"Not that either, idiot!" Laine said and snatched the bottle of wine away from her. "You drank it all?"

"Ah," Ella Rae said, pulling a bottle from the pocket of her coat. "But I came prepared."

"Thank God!" Laine said and rubbed her hands together while Ella Rae struggled with the cork.

Surely I had gone to sleep and was now dreaming. Laine and Ella Rae drunk while I was pregnant and trying to sleep? This had certainly been a season of firsts. I watched Ella Rae fumble with the cork for a full minute and a half before I said, "Corkscrew."

"YES!" Laine shouted. "Corkscrew!" Then she looked at me. "Do you have one?"

"Why yes, Laine," I answered. "I keep one in the pocket of my nightgown."

She looked so disappointed it made me laugh. "You really are a smart-ass, Carrigan."

"Wait!" Ella Rae ran out of my room and down the hall to hers. She was back in thirty seconds with her purse/suitcase. She flung it onto my bed, dug around a second or two, and produced a corkscrew.

"Why am I not surprised?" I asked.

"Voilà!" Ella Rae shouted as the cork hit the ceiling fan. She took a big gulp and passed the bottle to Laine. "I'm sorry you can't have any," she said to me.

"I'm good," I said. "Now what are we here to discuss?"

They looked at each other, clueless and intoxicated.

"Oh, I know!" Laine said. "My funeral. I want to plan my funeral."

"Yes!" Ella Rae said. "I knew it was something like that. This is good wine."

I stared at Laine. "You want to plan your funeral ... tipsy?"

She cocked her head. "Can you think of a better time?" she asked.

I had to give her that one. "Okay." I pulled a notebook and pen from the bedside table. "Knock yourself out."

She leaned back in the chair and took a big swallow of wine. "Okay, first of all, I don't want this big, weepy, drawn-out cry fest."

I continued staring at her.

"Write it down!" she demanded.

"Okay." I began writing. "No big, weepy, cry fest."

"No wailing or moaning," she continued.

"No wailing or moaning," I repeated.

"Hey, you've had that bottle for ten minutes," Ella said. "Give it back."

"I've had it all of thirty seconds!" Laine said.

I took the bottle from Laine and passed it to Ella Rae.

Laine pouted a moment but then continued. "There should be music, but not sad music."

"Music." I wrote it down. "Not sad."

"Well, maybe a little sad. I will be dead and all."

That drove a little dagger in my heart, and I bit my lip.

"Help me think of a good song," she said.

"I know!" Ella Rae said and began singing, "Ninety-nine bottles of beer on the wall, ninety-nine bottles of beer ..."

"Don't even look at her," I told Laine. "She's in her own kingdom over there."

"I think maybe ... hell, I don't know. You decide," Laine said.

I drew little circles on the paper in an effort to push this whole conversation from my mind.

"And I need you to deliver the emency, you know the eulory, the effigy, the—"

"Eulogy?" I asked, horrified at the thought.

"Yes! Bingo! Yahtzee! Booya!" Ella Rae hollered. "We remembered!"

"Yes," Laine said. "The eulogy."

I slammed the notebook shut. "Oh hell no! I can't do that!"

Laine waved me off. "Of course you can. Just tell them all who I am ... was. It'll be easy."

"You're fucking crazy, Laine!" I threw the notebook back into the drawer and slammed it.

"Ouch!" Ella Rae said, laughing. "Sister gal pulled out the f-word!"

Laine laughed with her and said, "Well, I'd do it my damn self, but I'll be the dead one!"

Ella Rae nodded nonchalantly. "She's gotcha there, Carri."

"Ella Rae, shut up! You aren't helping!"

"I wasn't trying to," she said. "Duh."

Laine had lost her mind. I couldn't stand in front of a church full of people and tell them who she was. Not without the wailing and weeping she'd just mentioned. I just couldn't do it. "Laine, maybe we should talk about this when we're, you know, maybe—"

"Do you think there's any more of this wine downstairs?" Ella Rae peered into the empty bottle.

"Ella Rae, please!" I said.

"Fine," she said and crossed her arms. "I'll wait for you to go back to sleep. You sure have been grouchy lately."

"Hormones," Laine stage-whispered behind her hand to Ella Rae and then looked back at me. "Listen, it ain't that big a deal. All you have to do is stand there and talk for ten minutes about all the wonderful traits I used to have … still have … you know what I mean. Whaddaya think, buddy?"

I shook my head. "You're drunk, that's what I think. And maybe we should discuss this tomorrow."

Laine looked at Ella Rae who was apparently counting something on the ceiling and snickered. Then she looked back at me, and I swear, in that one moment, she was sober as a judge. "Please say you'll do this for me. Nobody wants to talk about it. Me either. But I need to know you'll do this last thing for me."

Everything in me was screaming no, but I couldn't say it. She was right; it *would* be the last thing I would ever do for her. And I couldn't deny her that. I knew it was important to her to hear me say that I would do it, so I sighed and heard myself saying yes.

Laine smiled and stood up. "Come on, Ella Rae. We got what we came for."

"Where'd you put it?" Ella Rae said.

"Where'd I put what?" Laine said.

"Whatever it was we came for. Duh," Ella Rae said. "Y'all aren't thinking straight tonight. Now, *where did you put it?*"

"Oh! I think it's in my pocket." Winking at me, Laine shoved Ella Rae gently in front of her, looked back at me, and mouthed, "Thank you."

I faked a smile until the door closed behind them. I had rather somebody beat the hell out of me than deliver Laine's eulogy. How would I ever make anybody in that church understand who Laine Landry is? Was, rather. And what was I supposed to say? Here lies a chick that was so loyal she compromised her standards a thousand times to accommodate my lack of them? Was that too much information? How about, here lies a chick that loved McDonald's French fries but hated their burgers? Or, she loved Burger King burgers but hated their fries? How she had a heart for the underdog and a moral compass that would rival Mother Teresa? How could I ever explain how her words could cut me to the quick, but they'd always come from a place in her heart that I knew wanted the very best for me? How could I explain to anybody in ten minutes, ten hours, or even ten days what I had lost? What the *world* had lost? There were no tears that night; just an increasing alarm that the days were flying by, and they were taking Laine's life with them.

Much later, when Jack finally came to bed, I clung to him. The weight of what lingered on the horizon felt like a ton of bricks on my shoulders. I had avoided thinking about Laine's death, and I certainly avoided thinking about her funeral. When the thoughts pushed their way into my mind, I always pushed back. But the day was coming, and I was helpless to stop it. No matter how much I tried, no matter how much I fought, this was a battle I wasn't going to win. There would be a funeral, and even the guest of honor had embraced it.

Chapter 11

By the time early April rolled around, I was miserable for many reasons. Laine was slipping; I could see it happening every day. The changes weren't dramatic, but even small things alarmed me. The circles under her eyes seemed darker, her appetite wasn't as good as it had been, and she'd lost some weight. Maybe only five pounds or so, but it was noticeable. Her demeanor hadn't changed, though. She was still her cheerful self and quite excited about the arrival of the baby.

I, on the other hand, had gained twenty-two pounds and felt like a beached whale. Everyone, including my doctor, said that my weight was perfect, but I felt as clumsy as a cow and was sure I resembled one. I wondered all the time how other women did this four, five, and six times. This baby was doing a number on my body, and when I sat cross-legged in the bathtub, I felt like a Buddha statue. I would call the girls and Jack in to look at me.

I didn't especially like being pregnant anymore. It had been fun for exactly seven months. After that, it just pretty much sucked. Not to mention my boobies felt like rocks, I had to pee every thirty seconds, and if anyone looked at me sideways, I cried. That sounds shallow compared to what was happening to Laine, but it was true.

I was perched on a bar stool in the kitchen when Jack came in from outside and kissed my forehead. "Good morning, beautiful," he said and winked at me.

I made a face. "Whatever," I said. When he didn't respond, I said, "Do I disgust you?"

He picked up two of Mamie's famous cinnamon rolls, thick with icing and still warm, and put them on his plate. "You are more beautiful to me now than you have ever been," he said and took a big bite.

My mouth watered watching him eat, and I unconsciously peeled an orange. Just the smell of those rolls could pack five pounds on a person. I didn't dare eat one. Besides, I could bypass my mouth and just tape them to my butt and thighs. That's where they would go anyway.

"Don't even bother, Jack," Laine said, sipping orange juice and nibbling a piece of dry toast. "She won't believe a word you say."

"You didn't have to get a wench truck to pull you out of bed this morning," I said. "And there are mirrors in this house. I can see myself, you know."

"Carri, you are the perfect size," Laine said. "Even Dr. Davis says so. You look cute in your clothes, not all puffy and swollen. But I do wish you would wear something other than these sad-looking, faded overalls every day!"

"I can't help it," I said. "They're the only things that feel good." She was right, though. I wore them daily, and I was now two weeks into zero makeup at all. My hair was in a clip on top of my head, and I could see red curls springing in every direction. I probably should at least have brushed my hair. I turned to Jack again. "Really, do I disgust you?"

He smiled and patted my cheek. "I love you, sweet girl. See you at eleven." And out the door he went.

"See?" I said to Laine. "He can't even look at me for long."

She laughed. "Get over yourself. We're almost there!" She shoved her plate of toast and fruit away, even though she'd barely touched it.

"You didn't eat worth a damn, Laine," I said. "Are you feeling alright?"

She shrugged a little. "Most days."

That wasn't the answer I was looking for but was all I was going to get. I always wanted more, but those boundaries had been drawn a long time ago. I tried not to cross them, but once in a while, I did anyway. Sometime around Christmas I had asked her if she still thought nixing the chemo had been the route to take, and she'd gotten a little defensive with me.

"Look, Carrigan. It was my choice to make. And as soon as I made it, I had inner peace instead of that awful turmoil I had gone through for days. I didn't take the treatment because I didn't want my last days on earth to be spent sick, throwing up, and bald. I wanted to spend it appreciating and loving the people in my life. It may have bought me a little more time, but at what cost? I want to feel strong until this disease I didn't choose strips me of that. Not because a poison I *did* choose does it for me. I know you love me, and I know this hurts you. But please, don't question my decisions anymore. If there's something you need to know, I promise I will tell you." She wanted to fight the monster on her terms, and I grudgingly admired that. It was easy for me to say I'd have taken the treatment. I wasn't the one with the death sentence hanging over my head. From that day forward, I was careful to let her set the tone, even if it drove me insane. And it always, always did.

Not surprisingly, Laine changed the subject. "So, as cute as you look in your little overalls, will you please change clothes before we go to the doctor's office?"

I sighed. "Fine." I threw up my hands. "If you and Ella Rae can find me something to wear, I'll put it on."

An hour later, I had been pronounced fit to leave the house. I had to admit, I did look a lot better. I didn't like how the clothes clung to me, but they were stylish and cute, and I felt pretty, which did wonders for my attitude. I rolled my eyes at the thought. I'd turned into such a girlie girl lately. Jack had whistled at me when he came in, and I had blushed. Ugh, these freaking hormones. How embarrassing!

Jack had begun making the "OB run," as Ella Rae called it, with us when I started having to go weekly. When I was only going monthly, just the girls and I went, shopped, ate lunch, and made a day of it. But the closer it got, the more Jack hovered. We had watched a Lamaze DVD in our bedroom a few nights earlier of a baby being born, and I thought he was going to change his mind about the delivery room. I went into full panic.

"I don't think I can watch this, Carrigan."

"What do you mean?"

"I mean, maybe you should just let them put you to sleep and take the baby out." Jack looked a little pale.

"Jack! You watch cows give birth all the time! What is wrong with you?"

"It's not having the baby," he told me. "Do you hear her? I don't think I can listen to you do that."

I winced. I hadn't been too thrilled about the screaming either, and it was awfully sweet of him to be so concerned, but if he thought he was going to leave me in the delivery room, he was out of his mind. "I won't scream like that," I promised.

"You say that now," he said. "She probably said it too."

I laughed. My sweet Jack, who was tough as nails, didn't want to see me in pain. "I love you," I said.

"I bet you won't be saying that then," he said, pointing at the TV.

"Oh, I will too," I said and planted a kiss on his cheek. "It won't be that bad." I didn't believe a word of it, but it seemed to pacify him. Slightly.

"Let's roll, Team Whitfield!" Laine called. "Places to go, and people to see!"

My entourage was waiting in the driveway when I came down the porch steps. Jack jumped out of the driver's seat and held my hand while I got in the SUV. I rolled my eyes. "I hate this," I said, and he smiled. Truthfully, I really enjoyed being pregnant up until the last month. Now I felt awkward and clumsy, two things I had never felt in my life. I couldn't jog at all anymore, either. I kept feeling like I needed to hold my hands under my belly. I was ready for this baby to see the outside world. I highly commend and admire women who love being pregnant and want to have a baby every year, but I ain't one of them.

My OB-GYN, Dr. Ike Davis, was also Laine and Ella Rae's regular doctor. He was a sweet, jolly, older man with kind eyes and a heart of gold. He had a deer camp close to Bon Dieu Falls and was a college friend of Mr. Jack's and my daddy. He often came to the annual crawfish boil as well. I knew he felt awful about Laine. She had gone to him for her regular checkup barely a year before she'd been diagnosed with ovarian cancer. The checkup had revealed nothing abnormal. Laine knew that a regular exam wouldn't detect ovarian cancer, and she assured Dr. Davis that she understood that. He called the farm every week or two to check on her and had even stopped by a couple times. I knew her illness had broken his heart, and on some level, he felt some misguided responsibility, but Laine had never blamed him. Laine never blamed anybody.

"Here are all my favorite patients!" Dr. Davis said when he entered the exam room. He hugged each of us and shook hands with Jack. "How are you feeling, dear?" he asked Laine.

She playfully hit him on the shoulder. "Like pitching for the Saints!" she said.

He looked at me, puzzled.

"She thinks they play baseball," I explained.

He laughed. "Sometimes I wish they did." Then he smiled. "And how are you feeling, dear?"

"Like a busted can of biscuits," I said.

Dr. Davis laughed. "First time I've heard that one," he said. "But your chart looks great. You've only gained twenty-three pounds! And your blood pressure is perfect. I'm proud of you!"

"Yay," I said unenthusiastically.

"Please deliver this baby so her attitude will get better," Laine said.

"You been giving everybody a hard time?" he asked me.

"I have no idea what she means," I answered.

"Hmph!" Ella Rae grunted.

"Jack?" Dr. Davis said.

"Been a perfect angel," he answered.

"Ass kisser," Ella Rae said.

We all had a good laugh over that, including Dr. Davis.

"I need to utilize your pregnant-wife skills with some other husbands, Jack. Now let's take a look, shall we?"

I looked at Ella Rae, Laine, and Jack, all glued in their places. "Come on, y'all," I said. "At least look out the window till I get the damn sheet wrapped around me."

Ella Rae looked exasperated. "Is there anybody in this room who *hasn't* seen your cookie?"

Everybody looked at each other and then all looked back at me.

"Damn," I said and adjusted my feet in the stirrups.

It's one thing to go to the girl doctor by yourself, you know? It's uncomfortable, and it's always cold and always humiliating. But imagine if you had the doctor, his nurse, and three other people in the room with you. Yeah, I know. It was unusual, to say the least.

"How can you ask me to leave when I'll never witness anything like this again?" Laine had asked a couple weeks earlier when I'd hinted that they should leave before my exam.

I looked at her. "Really? Did you just play the death card so you could stay in here?"

She smiled smugly. "I did," she answered and was quite proud of herself, I think.

What could I do? There was no way I could talk Ella Rae into leaving if Laine was staying. Jack argued that he put the baby there in the first place, so he certainly wasn't going anywhere. So I lost that round, and from then on, everybody stayed. I guess I could've dragged people in off the street as well. Dr. Davis's rules seemed to fly out the window when we arrived. At least Jack had the good sense to turn his back during the actual exam. But I'm pretty sure the other two would've taken pictures if Dr. Davis had let them. I was actually afraid that they would ask and he'd say yes.

"Well?" Laine asked after the exam was completed.

"Well," Dr. Davis said. "Any time now."

I struggled to sit up and reached for Jack's hand. "What do you mean? I'm not due till next week!"

"Babies have a way of showing up whenever they want to." He smiled. "You're three centimeters dilated. You could stay there for hours or for days. Call me when you go into labor or when your water breaks. You have my cell number and home number, right?"

I bit my lip and nodded. Shit just got real.

Ella Rae was dancing up and down in place, and Laine was grinning from ear to ear. Jack was silent and squeezing my hand so hard it hurt.

I wiggled my hand around. "Ouch!"

"I'm sorry, baby," he said and picked my hand up and kissed it. "Better?"

I made a face at him. "What am I, five years old?"

"Next time I see you, we'll fetch a baby, okay?" Dr. Davis said.

"Okay," I said. "Thank you."

"Can I see you outside a minute, Doc?" Jack asked.

"Sure, Jack." Dr. Davis slid the door open. "Laine, you be sure and call me if you need anything."

"I will," she promised.

Dr. Davis and Jack disappeared into the hallway, and Laine and Ella Rae both started squealing and asking questions.

"Are you scared? Are you freaked out? Does it hurt? Can you feel it? What's it like?" They fired off round after round so fast I couldn't tell which one asked what question. But I could tell them for sure that the answer to each one was and emphatic yes!

"I just wasn't expecting him to say ... you know, I mean, I thought I had a week or two ... Yes, I am freaked the hell out!" I said.

"It's okay," Laine said and handed me my pants. "We'll be here, I promise!"

I was torn between a grateful heart because Laine would be there to see my baby, hold it, and love it and being so terrified that I found it hard to complete a sentence. I wasn't afraid of having the baby, but I was suddenly quite intensely aware that I would be its mother. What did I know about a baby? They had bobble heads and made puppy sounds. There. That was the extent of my knowledge on the subject. What had I been thinking? I hadn't been thinking at all! I couldn't be anybody's mother! I had just learned how to be a wife fifteen minutes ago! I'd been living in freaking la-la land for the past seven months. As long as the baby was inside me, I was mother of the year. But it was going to come out of me soon! My hands were shaking like leaves.

"I'm good," I lied and slipped my pants on. "It's all good."

"Great," Laine said. "'Cause I am starving! Let's eat."

That was music to my ears. Laine ate like a bird now and any admission of hunger sent us all scrambling to fetch food for her. The announcement also temporarily distracted me from worrying about dropping my baby the first time I held it or something worse. *Maybe I should read a book about babies*, I thought distractedly.

Jack was waiting on us in the parking lot, and we drove over to our favorite Mexican place, Simpaticos. We were seated at the table before I even thought to ask Jack why he'd spoken to Dr. Davis.

"What was that about?" I asked.

"Nothing," Jack said.

"Something," I corrected.

"I was just asking about anesthesia," he said. "Nothing special."

"What?" I laughed. "Are you serious?"

"Look, Carri," he said. "That DVD we watched was bad. It was bad!"

The girls and I began laughing.

"I don't want to take anything, Jack," I told him. "That's why we took Lamaze classes."

"We'll see," he said and took another gulp of his beer. "I'm just making a backup plan."

I shook my head. That was my Jack. He was always going to have a backup plan in place, no matter what was going on.

"Damn, Laine," Ella Rae said. "You don't have to lick the bowl. They'll bring you some more."

"Shut up, Rae," Laine said as she scraped the bottom of the salsa with a chip. "You complain if I don't eat, and you complain if I do."

"Excuse me." Ella Rae motioned for our server. "Can we have some more chips and salsa? Thank you." She turned to Laine. "Slow down, Porky. Help is on the way."

"They're just so good today," Laine said, licking her fingers. "Can I have yours?" she asked me.

I slid my salsa to her. I was almost giddy with excitement over her appetite. "Knock yourself out, girl."

"I feel great today," Laine announced. "Like I could run a marathon."

Ella Rae snorted. "Please! You wouldn't run thirty feet when you *didn't* have cancer!"

I guess in some circles that wouldn't have been politically correct. Even Jack raised an eyebrow. But in our circle, that was hilarious. Laine laughed so hard I thought she'd choke on her chips.

Jack shook his head. "You three have the most unusual relationship."

"Yes, we do," Laine said just as the fresh chips and salsa arrived. "Ah, finally!"

"So," Ella Rae said. "Let's talk baby names. And I want answers this time, not any of that 'we haven't decided' crap. It's bad enough you won't tell us what flavor it is."

"I don't *know* what flavor it is," I defended. I smiled and looked at Jack. "But Jack knows."

"What?" Ella Rae and Laine said in shocked unison.

"When did you find out?" Laine said, cramming her mouth full at the same time.

Jack smiled but remained silent.

"This is bullshit!" Ella Rae said. "Why does he get to know and we don't?"

"You know, Rae," I said, shrugging. "I don't know why my *baby daddy* should know and you shouldn't. He wanted to know, so he called, and Dr. Davis told him."

"That's so unfair," Laine said. "Wait ... I'm feeling faint." She grabbed her chest and rolled her eyes back in her head. "This could be it. I'm slipping ..." She looked at Jack. "That didn't work, did it?"

"Not even close," he said dryly.

"Please tell me you don't know, Carrigan!" Laine said.

"I don't, I swear," I promised. "And don't do that fake dying thing anymore. I don't like it. Jack won't even tell *me* what it is. I guess I could ask, but we're this close now, so I'll just wait."

Ella Rae looked at me like I was a stranger. "What's happened to you? Who are you? The whole time you've been preggers, you've either been pissed off or chilled like you're stoned. I never know what I'm gonna find in the mornings with you."

I laughed. "Have I been that bad?"

Nobody answered.

I laughed harder now. "Sorry! I thought I'd been a picture-perfect pregnant person."

"It's hot, it's cold, I want a Popsicle, I hate Popsicles, I'm sleepy, I can't sleep!" Ella Rae mocked.

"I'm hungry, I'm nauseous, it's too bright, it's too dark, I want pizza, I hate pizza," Laine continued.

I was cracking up, and so was Jack. "Stop!" I said. "I get it!"

"I'm never getting pregnant!" Ella Rae said. "It makes you a nut case."

"That ain't why," I said. "You can't leave alcohol alone for nine straight months."

"That is a lie!" she said.

"We all good here?" our server asked, appearing at the table.

"One more margarita," Ella Rae said, not even realizing what she'd done.

"SEE!" I shouted.

"Nothing says 'I mean business' like a shopping cart at the liquor store, Rae." Laine laughed. "I was mortified!"

"It was for a party!" Ella Rae defended.

"A party of one," I said.

"Okay." Ella Rae stopped laughing long enough to act offended. "Is this some kind of intervention? Because I gotta tell y'all, I am not an alcoholic. I just like to drink sometimes … and my favorite drink is called … a lot."

Laine spit iced tea out on the table, and I had to hold my belly under the baby to laugh. Jack just shook his head throughout the entire conversation.

Laine felt good, and she wasn't faking it. I could always tell when she faked it. There wasn't an imitation smile or reaction in her today. It was all authentic. She didn't look great, but she felt great, and I'd take that any day. We'd laughed so much the last hour and a half that I hadn't even thought of the cancer or what a terrible mother I was going to be. I looked at each face around the table, so happy and relaxed, and wished I could bottle and preserve it. I had wished that a lot lately.

"Enough!" Laine said, wiping the tea from the table. "Let's go buy something for the baby. Of course, if we knew if it was a boy or a girl, it would help the selection process tremendously!" She looked at Jack.

"Not a chance." He smiled.

"You are mean as a damn snake, Jack Whitfield," Ella Rae said as we gathered our things to leave.

I stood up and immediately felt a whoosh of warmth run down my legs. I stood still, looking at the puddle I was now standing in. "My water just broke," I said.

Leave it to Ella Rae to sum up a situation. "Oh *SHIT*!"

✷ *Chapter 12* ✷

"*P*ush, Carri, push!" Laine yelled in my ear. "You're almost there! Go! Go! Go!"

How much longer could this possibly go on? It felt like I'd been pushing for hours. If Jack or Laine told me to push one more time, somebody besides me would need a doctor tonight. At least Ella Rae wasn't trying to pull that rah-rah crap with me. The last time I saw her, she was gagging in the corner of the room. She always bugged out at the first sign of blood. I would've laughed if I weren't giving birth to what was surely an alien baby, biting its way into the world. I grit my teeth and pushed again, sweat dripping into my eyes, gripping Jack's hand so tight I thought his bones would break. The contraction finally subsided, and I flopped back down on the bed.

"Great job!" Laine cheered and patted my shoulder.

"Shut up, Laine, and get out of my face!" I yelled back.

"I know you don't mean that." She smiled and wiped my forehead.

"I do mean it! I swear I do!" I caught my breath, waiting for the next contraction that was about forty-five seconds away. I panted and tried not to watch the fetal monitor whose waves alerted me when another contraction started. Like I was going to miss it! I hated that damn monitor. Why, oh why, had I wanted to experience natural childbirth? It was like saying you wanted to experience someone peeling off your fingernails. Who says that and means it? Dr. Davis should've told me that I really wanted the epidural when I assured him repeatedly that I really didn't. This was excruciating. Surely something was wrong; this kind of pain couldn't be normal. Jack kissed my hand.

"Don't kiss me again! Not *ever*!" I snatched my hand away from him. But a contraction began, and I grabbed his hand back as quickly as I'd discarded it. I pushed for as hard and as long as I could until it was over and then once again fell back onto the bed.

"You're making progress, Carrigan," Dr. Davis encouraged me. "Don't quit on me."

"I can't push again," I told Jack, panting and trying again to catch my breath. "They're coming too fast. I'm too tired. I can't take another one. Please don't make me."

He looked so pained and pale I felt sorry for him. He kept telling me that I never had to do this again, that he never wanted to see me hurt this way again. That he'd get a vasectomy tomorrow—the best idea I'd heard in years. I even offered to perform it myself, only it involved a rusty hatchet and some rubbing alcohol. "It won't be long now, baby, I promise. Just try again, okay? Just a few more times."

"Go to hell!" I flung his hand away again and turned to Laine who was on my other side. "I know you have drugs in your purse, and I know what they are. Give me something, anything, please!"

Laine looked dumbfounded. "I can't give you cancer drugs!"

"Useless! Get out of my sight!" I said and turned back to Jack. The pained look on his face gave me some small amount of satisfaction. Good. I hoped he felt bad. It was certainly better than looking at Susie Sunshine on the other side. All Laine was missing was pompoms and a short skirt.

"If you will give me one more hard push, I promise you, I'll hand you a baby," Dr. Davis said.

I looked at Jack. "I can't, "I said. "Too tired. I can't do it again. Just let it stay in there."

"Look at me, baby," Jack said, wiping my face with his hands and kissing me. "You are the bravest, most beautiful girl I have ever known, and I love you so much. Please, just one more time, and then you can stop, I promise! Just one more."

I looked into his eyes, so full of love and concern. He was so good to me. Even when I didn't deserve it, he was good to me. But I still wanted to kill him. "Once more, and that's it!" I told him, through grit teeth. "That's it, you hear me?" I looked at the monitor; the contraction was almost here. I took a deep breath and prepared to push. I promised myself if it didn't happen this time, I would just die on this table, and I was remarkably alright with that. I shut my eyes tight, grit my teeth, and pushed harder than I knew I could. I could feel the scream through my clenched teeth before I heard it, felt the release I'd been working toward for so long, and then the relief as I collapsed on the bed. I had done it! I opened my eyes and saw tears rolling down Jack's face and heard Laine gasp in awe and Ella Rae hit the floor in a dead faint. Then I heard my baby cry.

"It's a girl!" Dr. Davis said. "A very mad little girl with a whole lot of red hair!"

"Is she alright?" I asked.

"She is perfect," Dr. Davis said. "Give me a couple of minutes, and she's all yours."

Jack, Laine, and I were crying while two nurses helped Ella Rae into a chair. We watched as they cleaned, weighed, and wrapped the baby up tight in blankets. Dr. Davis brought her to me and put her in my arms. "Congratulations, Mama and Daddy," he said. "She's an eight-pound beauty. You did good, Mama."

I couldn't even speak when he gave her to me. All I could do was stare at her. She was perfect indeed with pouty pink lips and a tuft of red hair. I knew as soon as I touched her that my life would never be the same, and I didn't want it to be. This soft little helpless creature wiggling and squirming in my arms tugged at my heart in a way I had never felt before. How could that happen after thirty seconds? Surely there was a stronger word for this than love. Holding her made me feel like I had come home after a very long trip that I hadn't really wanted to take.

I couldn't take my eyes off her. I hadn't even known I wanted her, but her existence somehow soothed me. My life up until that very moment seemed like a series of hits and misses. Then someone placed this gift I didn't deserve in my arms, and now my life made complete sense.

Just like that. I'd heard the word *miracle* thrown around all my life, but that night, my child changed my whole perspective on the world just by her entering it. If that wasn't a miracle, I didn't know what was.

I looked up at Jack who was clearly feeling a hail of emotions as well. I held her up, and he carefully took her from my arms. I'd only seen Jack cry once, when his grandfather died several years earlier. Watching him hold our daughter for the first time was one of the sweetest moments of my life. He hadn't yet said a word; I wasn't sure that he could. Just like me, he kept staring at her.

Ella Rae finally hobbled over to us and rolled her eyes. "I am *so* embarrassed," she said.

Laine and I both laughed, finally breaking up the tear festival.

"In the immortal words of Tommy Weeks," Laine said, "it ain't a party till somebody hits the floor."

"I just couldn't take all that grunting and pushing business!" Ella Rae said, shivering. "Whew! I'm glad that's over!"

"The show was tough on you, huh?" I asked, making a face. "You should've been in my seat."

Ella Rae laughed. "I was fine until that first … thing came out."

"What thing?" I asked.

"I don't know what that was," Ella Rae said, disgusted. "It was stuff coming out of you all night!"

"Tell me you didn't take pictures!" I was horrified.

"Take pictures?? Hell, I couldn't even look!"

"Thank God!" Ella Rae was the official photographer for that night, but I had told her repeatedly to not take anything that showed me in a less-than-flattering light. Meaning, don't snap pictures of my cookie.

"By the way, Carrigan," Laine said. "You had some pretty harsh words for me tonight. I was only trying to help."

"Seriously? I expected you to turn cartwheels any minute! You were like a Dallas Cowboys cheerleader. It was very annoying!"

"I actually thought at one point you were gonna take a swing at me." Laine laughed.

"Took too much energy," I said. "Or I would've."

"Look," Laine whispered and pointed to Jack and the baby by the window. He was holding her close to his face and whispering something we couldn't hear. She looked like she was watching him and that she understood very word. It was a beautiful sight, and Ella Rae thankfully had the presence of mind to snap a picture of it. I don't think Jack even realized she'd taken it. He just kept on whispering.

"I told you what kind of man Jack Whitfield is, didn't I?" Laine asked softly.

I smiled and wiped at the tears. "Yes, you did. You always did."

"Okay, okay," Ella Rae said. "That's enough *Little House on the Prairie* crap. Bring us the baby, Daddy!"

Jack walked over and handed her to Laine. "Hi, baby," she said.

I had to look away. I was intensely aware of this significant moment between my daughter and my best friend. "We have a name picked out," I finally said. "Jack, tell them." I didn't think I could get it out without blubbering.

"Ladies, meet Ella Laine Whitfield," Jack said.

Their jaws dropped. "Are you serious?" Ella Rae asked.

Laine pursed her lips together. I knew she was making a huge effort not to blubber too.

"We'll call her Elle," I said.

"Hi, Baby Elle," Laine said. "I'm your Aunt Lainie." She kissed her face lightly. "You are such a pretty girl. I love you already! I have so much I want to tell you." She paused and kissed her again. "So much to say but not so much time."

That cut us all like a knife. I was physically exhausted from the birth and emotionally and mentally exhausted by the explosion of feelings that flooded my heart and mind. I was still in awe at the wonder of Elle's birth just minutes earlier. She was just a promise, and suddenly, she was real and breathing and mine. Then I was crushed by the reminder of how fragile life is when Laine whispered to my daughter about time. One sentence spoke a thousand words when she told my child hello but echoed good-bye in the same breath. I knew that the bubble we'd been living in was delicate and precious, but I had never been as aware of it as I was that night.

"There are a lot of people outside waiting to meet you, little girl," one of the nurses said. "There must be thirty people out there!"

"Y'all better take her out there, Jack," I told him. I knew our families were dying to see her. They didn't even yet know that she'd arrived!

Laine gave the baby back to Jack, who held her close to my face for a kiss. "Tell Mommy we'll be right back. We just gotta meet some people."

I kissed her and adjusted the blanket around her little face. "Don't stay out there too long," I said. "And don't let everybody hold her. She's little, you know."

Jack smiled. "Already turned into Mama Bear?"

I smiled too. Where had that come from?

Jack slipped out the door to introduce our daughter to her family, to all the people who would love her and mold her and shape her into a woman one day. I could already imagine how loved she was going to be. My heart was so filled with gratitude that I thought it would pop right open. But Laine's words to my baby played over and over in my mind. "Not so much time." It was heartbreaking as well as heartwarming. The conflict of emotions was too much for me, and once again, I began to cry.

Dr. Davis stood by my bed and put his hand on my arm. "I know what you're thinking, but it's a happy time, Carrigan," he said softly. "Don't look down the road right now. Just look at today. She's a beautiful, healthy baby. Concentrate on what you have."

I shook my head. "Thank you, for everything," I said.

"You're welcome." He patted my shoulder. "They will get you to a room shortly, and I'll be around in the morning to check on you."

I closed my eyes and tried to follow his advice. He was right, of course. There was so much to be thankful for. And I was thankful.

Much later that night, I woke up and realized I had managed to hold onto that thought. I opened my eyes to see Jack sitting by the window holding Elle and telling her what a big world there was outside. He told her there were ponies to ride and wagons to pull and puppies to love. But my favorite thing he said was "Daddy waited a long time for you, little girl." I drifted back to sleep happier and more at peace than I'd been in a very long time.

Chapter 13

Six weeks later, I was longing for those peaceful nights we'd had at the hospital. Elle was a good baby during the day. She nursed, stayed awake for a little while, and then slept again. She had quickly become the light and center of my life. But every night at two a.m., the house became the site of the Nightly Colic Festival, and the whole house got up for the party. We didn't really have another choice. I don't know where the child got her set of lungs, but they were strong, I assure you. Most nights, I had to fight someone else to hold her. Everybody had their own version of what would work, and of course, none of it did, but they tried. Mr. Jack usually took the first swing, walking her around, showing her pictures and telling her stories. Then Mrs. Diane would take her into the parlor and play the piano while Elle sat in the bouncy chair. That was shortly followed by Laine, who would sing every children's song known to man. Ella Rae never took a turn but instead sat miserably in a chair and marveled at the volume of Elle's screams. Jack thought taking her on the porch was the magic trick, and when I finally got to hold her, I rocked her and waited it out. Some nights, they all tried to send me back to bed. Finally, one night, I took them up on the offer.

I lay in bed thinking about how drastically my life had changed. Just a year ago, I was running around, chasing my tail, looking for something and not knowing what that something was. I had been scared to death Jack would make a fool out of me before I could make a fool out of him. Why had we ever let ourselves get to that point? I never asked him what happened to make him push me away. But one night, just after we'd all moved in at the farm, he'd brought it up himself. We were lying in bed when he suddenly turned to me and said, "I'm sorry."

"Sorry for what?" I asked.

"Sorry for what happened to us," he answered.

"It doesn't matter," I said to him, and I meant it.

"I know it was my fault." He wrapped his arms around me. "I am responsible for anything either of us did."

I turned over to face him. "That's not true, Jack. We all make our own choices."

"I should've known better." He continued like I hadn't spoken at all. "But you were so young. I started feeling like I had taken your youth away from you. I knew then it was unfair. And the truth is, I didn't want anybody else to have you. But later ... I ... I just had to let you choose. So I backed off."

"But Jack, I had already chosen!" I protested. "I chose you!"

"I know," he said. "But at the time, all I could think about was how I'd taken your youth away from you, and that one day you'd resent me for it."

I sat up in bed and took his face between my hands. "You didn't take anything from me. You gave me the world! Don't you know that?"

He smiled. "I know that now," he said.

"We don't have to do this," I told him. "It doesn't matter to me anymore. I'm where I want to be. Where I always wanted to be. With you. I love you. Always."

I wondered if I would ever know the full story of why he "backed off" as he put it. But the full story didn't interest me at all, only the rest of the story did. I hoped we would never speak of it again.

Being at the farm was like being safely tucked away in our own little corner of the world, like being wrapped in a cocoon where nothing and no one could ever touch us. I rarely even made the trip into Bon Dieu Falls anymore, and when I did, it was brief and necessary. I was completely and totally wrapped up in this life and with my people. All I needed was already here, and nothing could hurt, bother, or threaten us. Of course, that was nothing more than an illusion I clung to like a life raft. I shuddered to think that one day something bad was going to happen, and I knew it was coming sooner rather than later.

Laine was sicker. A lot sicker. She hid it when she could, but it was becoming obvious. She was frail and in pain more than she had been. She only talked about her medical issues with Debra, so there was no use questioning her, but there was no ignoring it either. She took her meds and napped more often and ate less. She'd lost interest in most everything except Elle and whatever she did in her bedroom when she disappeared for hours at a time.

Ella Rae and I asked her over and over if she wanted to go back to the hospital at least for a checkup with Dr. Rougeau, but she always declined. "For what?" she'd ask. "What's he gonna do? Take an X-ray and tell me I'm dying?" So we'd let the subject alone.

Laine seemed to be having a little difficulty breathing at night, so Jack bought her a bed that inclined. She said it helped, but you never really knew. Debra kept a close eye on her, and I think probably all of us checked on her during the night. Mrs. Jeannette had begun sleeping over more often as well. Between Laine and Elle, nobody really slept anymore. We just all catnapped until daylight and started all over again.

Since last summer, when we found out I was pregnant, we had started taking tons of pictures of everything and everybody. It had been Laine's idea. She wanted the baby to have pictures of her. Many nights, when the rest of the house was trying to sleep or entertaining Elle, I would spread the pictures out on my bed and look at them. Laine wanted me to pick out my favorites so we could use them at her funeral.

Discussing her funeral had become much like planning a holiday these days. She, Ella Rae, and I talked about it freely since the night Laine had asked me to give her eulogy, something I still wouldn't allow myself to think about. Laine was adamant about not letting anyone see her after she'd passed. It was alright for us, her family, to tell her good-bye, but after that, she wanted us to "slam that thing shut. It won't be me anyway. I'll be in heaven." I wished I could find comfort in that, but I didn't. I also wished I could find the comfort in God that Laine found, but I couldn't. I was still mad as hell at God.

When my mother would ask me how I was doing regarding Laine's illness, she would always tell me to pray about it. But I couldn't pray. Not even after Elle was born, and I knew she was a blessing, a heaven-sent blessing. I was thankful for her, but I wanted nothing to do with God. All my life, I had been taught that everything happens for a reason, that something good always comes from something bad, and that God's timing is always perfect, even if we didn't understand it. And I had accepted that. After all, I had lost the grandparents I loved so much and aunts and uncles and had grieved for each of them. But they had lived their lives. That was the way it was supposed to happen. Not like this. Not snatched out of the game in the fourth inning.

What possible reason could God have for taking Laine? She was a gift to everyone who knew her, not just to Ella Rae and me. The children she'd taught in the past still loved her. They'd run up to her to say hello everywhere we went. She was a huge part of our church, not a sporadic part of it like I was. She was kind and gentle and wise. So how could God justify this move? And how was I ever to forgive Him for it? I was raised in the Deep South where God, country, and family were the other holy trinity. My parents had taken me to church all my life, and after I grew up, I went on my own, even if it was hit and miss. But I was beginning to question all those things that had been drilled into me since I was small. Was it truly all part of some grand design? And if it was, was God sitting up in the sky with a clipboard and a red pen, keeping score and rolling dice? You live, you die, and you I haven't yet decided on? Or was it all just some huge random craps shoot and when we died it was over? I truly didn't know what I believed anymore.

I picked up a picture of Laine swinging around a column on the front porch. It had been taken in the fall of last year. I knew because all the mums were blooming in the background. She had a huge smile on her face and looked like the picture of health. She looked happy too. Really happy. I examined it closely. It had captured her perfectly, the very essence of her. This was the picture we'd use as the centerpiece at the funeral. I'd have it enlarged and framed, and we would place it on the table beside her at church. The tears that came so freely to me now spilled down my face, and I didn't even really notice them or bother to wipe them away. They were nearly as natural as breathing these days, and I had accepted them as normal. I sat the picture on my nightstand and flipped off the light, very aware of the significance of the decision I'd just made.

When I woke up, it was ten a.m. I couldn't believe I had slept that long. I would've probably slept longer too, but my milk had soaked my shirt. Whoever was the winner of the "I'm Holding Elle" contest must've used frozen breast milk.

I went downstairs in search of my family but couldn't find a soul, not even Mamie. But I could hear laughter coming from the porch and followed the sound. I peeped out the bay window and laughed. They had a regular living room set up outside. Elle's bassinet, Laine's chaise, and Mrs. Diane's settee from the sun porch were all on the big porch, which was well shaded and kept cool by the outdoor ceiling fans. The tea service beside the front door was full of Mamie's pastries and her signature cinnamon rolls. I reached for one but thought better of it and put it back. I only had five pounds of baby weight left to lose, and I was determined to get rid of it. I poured a cup of tea, skipped the sugar, and went outside.

"Good morning, Mommy!" Mrs. Diane said and turned Elle around so I could see her.

"Good morning, my baby!" I put my tea down and took her from her grandmother. I still fell in love with her every morning as soon as I saw her. I kissed her little pouty baby lips and nuzzled her neck. She smelled so good. How did I ever do something this right?

I walked to the end of the porch and into the morning sun, careful to shield her eyes. It was a beautiful morning; the sky was a bright and brilliant blue. Elle scrunched her little body and made those baby grunt sounds I loved so much. It was the middle of May, and the temperatures were still in the lower eighties. I loved this time of year, but I knew it wouldn't be long before the Louisiana humidity would make it impossible to sit out here with the baby. For the thousandth time in the last few months, I wished I could freeze the moment.

"Okay," Laine's voice said behind me. "You've said good morning to her. Now bring her to me."

I kissed my baby again and walked back to the others. "Let's go see Lainie," I said. I looked down at Laine, smiling and holding her thin arms out to cradle Elle. I bit my lip. Dear God, she looked bad. She was so thin, and the circles under her eyes were deeper and darker. I placed Elle in her arms and sat down on the chaise beside them.

"How are you this morning?" I asked her.

"I'm fine," she lied.

She was breathing harder and harder every day, and this morning it seemed to be a particular struggle. I wanted to breathe *for* her and instinctively took a deep breath and sighed. I suspected the cancer was in her lungs now. She had begun coughing quite a bit a couple weeks earlier, especially at night. She had practically stopped eating anything at all too. Mamie gave her meal replacement shakes that were very high in calories and vitamins, but she rarely finished one. She had promised us months before that when the cancer became too much and too painful for her, she would ask Debra to sedate her. But until then, if she could stand it, she wanted to be aware. She wanted to let nature do what nature did. Her resolve continued to amaze me, but I still wished for more time and wished she had taken the chemo. But she was doing this her way and on her terms. That way, she explained, when her life ended, she'd really have won the war because she'd done it the way she'd chosen. That the cancer she hadn't chosen and the chemo poison she'd refused had robbed her of nothing except time.

We sat in silence for a while, enjoying the morning, the smell of freshly cut hay, the sound of birds singing, and Elle's baby sounds. It was that kind of unflawed, companionable silence that could only be enjoyed by people so close where words weren't necessary. A smile, a touch, or a look sometimes said more than words ever could anyway. It was a beautiful morning indeed.

Laine and Elle had fallen asleep, and I reached over to pick up the baby. Elle did her little baby scrunch again, arms over her head and legs doubled up beneath her, that made me feel like she had just accomplished some incredible feat when in reality all she did was stretch. I was still sure my daughter scrunched better than any other baby in the world.

Laine stirred slightly. "Is she asleep?" she asked.

"She is," I said. "I didn't mean to wake you."

"No," she answered. "It's fine. I need to talk to you and Ella Rae anyway."

Mrs. Diane stood up and took Elle from me. "You girls stay on the porch and chat," she said. "My granddaughter and I have things to do, don't we, sweet girl?"

I kissed Elle's hand and sat back down on the edge of Laine's chaise. Ella Rae pulled her chair closer to us.

"Whatcha got, girl?" I asked.

Laine took a short breath and looked at both of us a moment before she spoke. "It can't be much longer now, right? Maybe a week or two. If that."

Ella Rae began to cry, and I bit my lip until I tasted blood.

"It's okay, y'all," Laine said. "Really, it is. It's kind of a relief. I'm tired … and I'm ready. Almost."

I didn't reply, and Ella Rae grabbed Laine's hand but stared out across the field.

"We knew this was coming," she said softly. "Please, don't get all weird on me now. You both promised."

I shook my head and swallowed. Of course we knew it was coming. The knowledge permeated every hour of every day. But knowing it was coming certainly did nothing to lessen the anxiety or soften the blow.

"Answer me," Laine said, a little louder now.

"Yes," I said, trying not to choke on the words. "We knew it was coming. What can we do? What do you need?"

Laine tugged at the afghan in her lap and seemed to struggle over her words. "Look," she said finally. "I don't know if this is right or wrong. And I don't even know if I should do this. But … I think I'd like to see Mitch. Do you think that would be possible?"

"I don't know, Laine," I answered, surprised. "But we'll surely do what we can to find him."

Ella Rae dabbed at her eyes and turned around to face us. "He's in

Dallas," she said. Laine and I stared at her. She shrugged. "The Internet is a wonderful thing."

"When—?" Laine began to ask.

"I started looking for him the day after you told us," Ella Rae confessed a bit sheepishly. "I kept it to myself because you said you didn't want to see him. But I kept thinking that maybe you'd change your mind."

I shook my head. "You sneaky little shit! I didn't know you had it in you to keep a secret that long!"

Ella Rae smiled. "I learned from the master."

I laughed; she got me on that one. I glanced over at Laine who looked a little flushed, but in a good way. She was smiling too.

"What did you find out?" she asked. "Do you think he would come if I called him? Or maybe you could get an e-mail address?"

Ella Rae looked down at her feet. "There's more, Laine." She said looking sheepish again.

"What is it?" Laine asked, alarmed. "Is he okay?"

Ella Rae looked up, her eyes brimming with tears. "No," she answered. "I mean, yes, he's okay, but ... I sorta ... well, I already talked to him."

"What?" I couldn't believe she hadn't said mentioned a word of this to me.

She shrugged again. "Nobody said I couldn't call him. He wants to see you, Laine. He's wanted to for a long time. Even before I called."

Stunned, Laine said, "Swear!"

"I swear," Ella Rae said. "He said he would be by the phone, waiting for my call." She pulled a piece of wrinkled paper out of her pocket. "See? I keep his numbers with me all the time. Work, cell, and home."

"But if he wanted to see me, why hasn't he tried in all these years?" Laine was skeptical, but I could still hear excitement in her voice. "I mean, Bon Dieu Falls isn't a huge place."

"He figured you were married now, with a house full of kids," Ella Rae answered and looked away again. "He didn't want to disrupt your life."

"And?" Laine asked.

"What do you mean, 'and'"? Ella Rae said.

"I mean, what are you not telling me?" Laine asked.

"That's it." Ella Rae shifted in her chair. "He has no family left here, no ties, no way of knowing anything about you. That's it." Again, she shifted in her chair.

That wasn't it, though. I knew it, and Laine knew it too. Something about Ella Rae's tone and body language belied her words. We knew each other too well for this.

"Rae," Laine said. "Don't make me beg. Please."

Ella Rae sighed heavily and took Laine's hand in hers. "Mitch and his wife divorced about a year and a half ago. He said the marriage had always been rocky, but he stayed for his son. And by the way, that is the only child he has. But he's always thought about you and wondered where you were and what you were doing. He never forgot you, Laine."

Ella Rae paused for a second, but Laine urged her to continue. "Come on, Rae. Just say it, whatever it is."

"He came looking for you last year," Ella Rae blurted out and started to cry in earnest then. "It was the same time you'd gotten sick, and we were all at the hospital. He couldn't find anyone he knew around here, and he ran into Jeff Nealy at the post office. Jeff told him what had happened."

Laine's lip began to tremble. I took her other hand in mine.

"He was crushed, Laine," Ella Rae continued. "And I could hear it in his voice. He even went to the hospital and sat in the lobby for two days. He even saw Carrigan and Jack in the parking lot one day but couldn't bring himself to ask."

Laine started crying then too, and I got mad as usual. What a goddamned Greek tragedy this had turned into.

"In the end, he thought it would be worse on you if he showed up then, so he went back to Dallas." Ella Rae was nearly sobbing now. "I'm so sorry. Please don't be mad at me! You said you didn't want to see him. But then when I talked to him, I didn't know what to do."

Laine shushed her. "Ella Rae, I'm not mad at you. You respected my wishes." She dabbed at her tears. "This is just all … such a shock. So … so …"

"Unbelievable," I offered and handed Laine the box of tissues from the wicker table beside us.

"Yes," she said. "The perfect word."

"I wanted to tell you," Ella Rae said. "But he begged me not to." Ella Rae was truly in anguish. "Not until you asked for him. He texts me every day and asks how you are."

Laine closed her eyes tightly, digesting the information.

"I'm so sorry, Laine," Ella Rae said again.

"There is nothing to be sorry about," Laine assured her.

This was hard to watch. It had to be gut-wrenching for Laine. Just the "what might have been" part of it was breaking my own heart. She was getting screwed out of a life and now she'd gotten screwed out of ever having the one man she ever loved. I wanted to scream for her and for me.

Laine gathered her composure and then looked over at me. "How do I look?" she asked.

I pursed my lips. "The truth or a lie?"

"Truth," she said. "Always."

I shot the arrow. "You are still beautiful," I told her. "And you look like you are fighting a really hard battle right now."

Ella Rae stood up. "He knows the score, Laine. He understands what's going on."

"And Laine," I said. "You really are still beautiful."

Ella Rae got her phone from her pocket. "The text has been written for weeks," she said. "All I have to do is hit send."

Laine drew in a long, deep breath. "Send it," she said.

Chapter 14

"Hold still!" I said.

"I'm trying to," Laine said. "But you're pulling my hair!"

"Because you won't sit still!"

"Why won't you let me look in the mirror?"

"Because I'm not finished," I told her for the tenth time. "And just so you know, your hair is gorgeous. Looks just like it always did."

She smiled and winked. "And I kept it too."

I smiled but didn't answer. We had never exactly seen eye to eye on the chemo thing, so I didn't comment on remarks like that. I certainly wasn't going to stir any pots that day.

Mitch had answered Ella Rae's text message three days earlier in less than thirty seconds and would be there within the hour. The mood in Laine's bedroom that morning was euphoric. We'd even gotten her to eat a few bites of scrambled eggs at breakfast and a whole piece of toast and drink half her juice. That itself was cause for celebration.

My mother had picked Elle up earlier and had taken enough frozen milk to last the whole day. We'd run everybody else out of the house so Laine and Mitch could be alone. But Ella Rae and I were staying, just in case she needed us. We'd decided to make a day of it on the sun porch.

"Purple or blue?" Ella Rae asked and held up two shirts.

"Purple," Laine and I said in unison.

"Great minds," I said, laughing.

"I'm gonna start your makeup." Ella Rae pulled up a chair in front of her. "Don't whine."

"I'm not gonna whine!" Laine whined.

"See?" Ella Rae said. "You have done this our whole lives! Somebody comes at you with a powder puff, and you automatically start."

"Fine," Laine said. "I won't talk at all."

"That would be great," Ella Rae told her.

"Did you hear that, Carrigan?" Laine asked.

"You just talked," Ella Rae scolded. "Now close your mouth, and let me work."

Fifteen minutes later, I pronounced her perfect. "You may turn around now." I spun her around in the swivel chair to face the mirror.

"Wow," she said softly. "I don't even look sick anymore! My eye circles are gone too! I look amazing!"

I turned so she wouldn't see my expression. She did look amazing. Her hair was still thick and beautiful, and Ella Rae had done a great job camouflaging her hollow cheekbones and the dark circles under her eyes. But she was so thin that it startled me. Debra had begun helping her bathe a few weeks ago and dress in the mornings and undress at night, so I hadn't seen her without clothes until this morning. Her bones protruded under her skin so badly that it made me want to gasp. I looked over her head at Ella Rae and knew she was thinking the same thing.

"You look beautiful," I said.

"You do," Ella Rae confirmed. "Now come on. It's getting close. Let's get you dressed."

I had made a flying trip to Shreveport and bought three different outfits for her. I knew she'd want jeans, so I got different styles in each pair and shirts and summer cardigans in every color I could find. She chose a pair of jeans with rhinestone pockets and a lavender top with a purple cardigan. She'd always worn a size eight. I had bought a size zero, and they were a little loose. But she looked pretty, and more importantly, she felt pretty, and that made all the difference.

I heard Mr. Jack's dogs barking and looked at my watch. Mitch was right on time. We walked into the living room, and Laine sat on the sofa. She was beaming. I fluffed her hair, gave her a quick hug, and met Ella Rae at the door to greet Mitch Montgomery.

"Hey," Laine said as Ella Rae reached for the front door. "Thank you both. For everything. I don't know what I'd do without you."

I smiled and felt the now-familiar lump in my throat. "Well, lucky for you, you never have to find out."

Ella Rae walked out on the porch and waited as Mitch walked up the driveway. He was taller than I remembered, and his hair was short now but still curly. He was a very handsome man. He stepped onto the porch and extended his hand. "Carrigan," he said. "You look exactly the same."

I smiled at him and took his hand. "Thank you, and I wish that were true. I'm glad you're here, Mitch."

He looked over at Ella Rae. "May I hug you?" he asked.

Ella Rae opened her arms and hugged him.

"I can never thank you enough for calling me," he said, his voice thick with emotion. "I'll never be able to repay you."

Ella Rae cried, of course. I was getting a little weepy myself.

"I just wish it could've been sooner," Ella Rae told him. "She's awfully weak."

He looked worn and worried. "I have a lot of regrets, ladies. If I could go back and do things differently ..."

"Stop," I said. "We all have things we'd like to take back or do over, I assure you. It doesn't matter. You're here now." I couldn't believe I said that to Mitch Montgomery. Just a few months earlier, I wanted to strangle him with my bare hands in front of God and everybody. But I knew what regret felt like. I knew how it felt to do something you wished you could take back. Besides, he was here to make our girl happy, if only for a little while. And that was good enough for me.

"She's in the front room on the sofa," Ella Rae said. "Go on in."

Ella Rae and I sat on the porch swing when he went inside. Before long, we could hear muffled crying from both of them. It was sweet and awful and heartbreaking all at once. I was dying to look in the window, but I knew that would be a terrible thing to do. Ella Rae must've read my mind because she was suddenly racing to the window.

"I can't help it," she said. "I have to see!" She peered into the window. "Awww ... Carri, come look!"

It was killing me not to see what was happening. I ran over to the window and looked in. Laine and Mitch were wrapped in an embrace with Laine practically in his lap. I couldn't see her face, but his was twisted in tears and regret. It's funny how you can read things on people's faces when you've been through a lot. My heart ached for him. He'd done the right thing years ago and gave up the person he loved to be with the ones who needed him. I had to respect him for that. He loved Laine, which was evident. Maybe he'd gone about it all wrong, maybe it hadn't started under stellar circumstances, but I was certainly not in a place to judge anybody's decisions. Mitch and I were a lot alike. He'd ended up in the arms of the love of his life, and so had I. Only I had gotten the fairy tale, and he'd gotten the Greek tragedy. Life could be so beautiful and yet so cruel.

"Come on," I told Ella Rae, grabbing her hand. "This isn't our moment."

We walked back to the porch swing, her hand still in mine. I was so grateful that Mitch had come. Seeing Laine actually excited this morning was such a comfort. She had ... I looked down. "What the hell is wrong with your hands, Ella Rae?"

"What do you mean?"

"It's like holding sandpaper!" I said. "What have you done?'

She rubbed them together and made a face. "They do feel rough."

"Use some lotion! And don't touch me with them again!"

Jack walked up the steps about the same time Ella Rae began rubbing her hands all over my face.

"Stop it, sandpaper girl!" I said, trying to slap her hands off me.

"What are y'all doing?" Jack asked, stopping in front of us.

"Feel her hands, Jack! Touch him, Rae."

She moved her hands up and down Jack's arms.

"Damn, girl," he said. "You been using sandpaper on those hands?"

"See?" I said.

Jack headed to the door, and Ella Rae and I both shouted, "No!"

"What?" he said, taking his hand off the door handle.

"Laine and Mitch are inside, remember?" I asked. "You can't go in."

"I'm thirsty," he said. "Can I go through the sun porch?"

"No!" we shouted again.

"Well, damn," he said. "What am I supposed to drink?"

Ella Rae pointed at my chest. "Drink from the fountain of homogenized."

I slapped her hand as Jack laughed. "She assures me regularly that those are for the baby."

"Go drink out of the hose," I told him.

"Damn," he said again. "Maybe the boys have something in the barn." He started back down the steps and popped my backside. "You look good today, Mama."

I smiled. "Hurry home."

"Let me know how that goes." He gestured toward the house.

"I will," I told him.

"Now," I said, folding my arms. "If you're gonna sit here, don't touch me with those Brillo pads."

Ella Rae laughed. "Fine," she said and tucked her hands under her thighs. "Carri," she said, suddenly serious. "Do you ever wonder what it will be like … later?"

"After she's gone, you mean?" I asked, but I knew exactly what she meant

"Yes."

"I think about it all the time," I confessed. "I try not to, but I do. Do you think about it?"

She nodded. "All the time."

"It's strange to think about the future without her, isn't it?" I said.

"I don't even know *how* to think about it without her."

"It's like it upsets the balance, tips the scales or something," I said. "Who's gonna keep the score at ballgames? Who's gonna put together our electronics? Who's gonna tell me my jeans are too tight?"

"Who's gonna dip the Martha Washington balls at Christmas?" Ella Rae continued. "Who's gonna drive us around while we drink?" And then she smiled. "But I guess Baby Elle has put a kink in that, hasn't she? Who's gonna be the responsible one now?"

We both laughed at our ridiculous questions and at ourselves, but we laughed to keep from crying. The truth was, Laine's absence was going to leave a huge hole in our lives. What would happen when a third of our lifetime trio was no longer here? We'd starred in the Carri, Laine, and Rae Show for so long, I wasn't sure Ella Rae or I would have any identity later. We fed off each other so much that losing Laine would be like losing an arm or a leg. Life would certainly go on, I knew that, but life as we'd known it would not.

Several years earlier, we'd lost a classmate in an automobile accident. We'd gone to school with him all our lives. His name was Ricky Cahill. We weren't really close friends, but we were all on friendly terms with him. And in small towns, you show up at wakes and pay your respects. He was a friendly guy, outgoing and good-looking. I remember thinking at his wake how awful and tragic this was. I also remembered something Laine had said that night sitting on the church pew beside me. "I know this is sad," she'd said, "and I get that, I'm sad, too, especially for his family. But I keep hearing people say he had his whole life in front of him, and I guess he did. But isn't what you leave behind the important thing? He was a great guy; everybody loved him. That's an amazing way to be remembered. What difference does it make how long you live?" I don't know what made me think of that sitting on the porch swing, but it brought me some measure of comfort. Laine would leave this world having made a difference. I knew that from the students who were in and out of the farm all the time to see her. I knew it because the mailbox was stuffed with cards every time the mail ran. Her life, as brief as it would be, had touched countless others. I was both proud of and grateful for that.

I also knew Laine wasn't afraid to die. While my faith had been shaken by her illness, hers had been bolstered. She spoke of heaven as if she'd seen it already. She could see her daddy and grandparents again and a cousin she'd lost. Even pets. She said as soon as she closed her eyes, she'd be in the presence of God, which was why she didn't want the casket open. "I don't want people looking at me and remembering me like that. They will see a shell and feel sorry for me, and I'll already be in paradise. It makes no sense." She had the blind faith of a child, and I wished I had half of it.

"Do you think she'll save us a seat?" Ella Rae asked.

It took me a moment or two to realize what she meant. "Where? In ... heaven?" I asked.

"Yes," Ella Rae said. "You know, I'm just saying ..."

"Oh, sure she will, Rae," I answered sarcastically, "because she so loves to do that. Here's a direct quote: 'If y'all could get your asses anywhere on time, I wouldn't have to save seats every time we attend a function. Oh, wait! Let me guess! Did Ella Rae stop for a drink and get in a fight? Or did you find an attractive man that can't spell?' Remember that?"

Ella Rae laughed. "I do remember that! She said it at church!"

"On the front pew," I confirmed.

"Do you ever wonder what she does in her room all the time?"

"I do. And it's driving me crazy! But every time I ask her, she just says she's working on a project."

"I went in her room the other night to get her a sweater and tried to snoop around a little," Ella Rae confessed. "But damn Debra walked in and just stared at me. I felt like I was at school and got caught smoking again!"

I suddenly felt my breasts begin to sting and knew it was meal time for my sweet Elle. I needed to pump. "Crap! I forgot to get my breast pump out of the kitchen."

Ella Rae made a face while I held my hands against my chest. "Do you have any idea how disgusting that is?" she asked.

"It's not disgusting. It's natural."

"It's appalling!" Ella Rae said.

"What do you think they're there for, Ella Rae? And when did you find out what *appalling* meant?"

"I read sometimes, smart-ass! And I think they are decorative. You know, like Christmas ornaments."

I shook my head. "I have to get my pump. This stuff is liquid gold. I can't waste it." I pressed my hands tighter against my chest.

"Don't you have them maxi pads in there?"

"What?"

"Didn't you stick the maxi pads in your bra?" Ella Rae repeated. "You always do."

"Ella Rae, they are not maxi pads," I explained. "They are *breast* pads."

"Thick, white, poofy. Same thing," she said.

I shook my head. "I cannot *wait* for you to have a baby."

"I hope you don't think I'm gonna feed it with my boobies," she said indignantly. "Besides, that's why doctors give dry-up shots and Walmart makes bottles. Now keep those things away from me!"

"You are crazy," I told her. "Now go look in the window, and tell me what they're doing. Maybe they won't notice us."

Ella Rae crept over to the window and gestured for me to come as well.

My curiosity had gotten the better of me this time, and I peered into the living room. Laine and Mitch were still on the sofa, but lying down now. Mitch had pulled Laine against him, and I was pretty sure she was asleep. Mitch was gently stroking her hair and looking down at her. He stopped briefly to wipe his tears and then began stroking her hair again. When he saw Ella Rae and me, he silently mouthed, "Thank you."

I grabbed Ella Rae's hand, not minding the sandpaper this time. We'd just witnessed an extraordinarily sweet moment. The last few months had been full of them, and I was grateful for them all. Laine would die in peace with everything and everybody now. What a rare and incredible blessing.

Chapter 15

*M*itch had stayed with us for the next five days. He met Mrs. Jeanette, Michael, Michael's wife, and family. Ella Rae had told them who Mitch was. I don't know if they were shocked by his presence, but they accepted him immediately and thanked him profusely for coming. He made friends with Jack and Tommy too. They tried to make him feel as at home as possible, offering to take him places and show him things, but he didn't take them up on it too much. He stayed by Laine's side for most of those five days. Although Laine became more and more emaciated, I'd never seen her smile so much.

I had grown to like Mitch and had come to understand his decision to leave Laine years ago. I assured him that an explanation wasn't necessary, but he insisted on sharing the story with Ella Rae and me. During those days, I began realizing that there is no easy way to understand anyone's choices until we've walked in their shoes. Mitch had decided to put his child's needs before his own. Maybe before I had Elle that wouldn't have resonated with me. The truth is, as Mitch talked and I looked down at my sleeping baby in my arms, his decision made absolute sense. He married his ex-wife because she was pregnant, not because he loved her. But he thought that maybe he could grow to love her, and that his decision was the right one at the time.

Mitch tried to make the marriage work, but from the beginning, it didn't. His wife accused him of cheating constantly, which caused frequent and violent arguments that usually ended with her taking their son and going to her mother's house for days at a time. But he had always remained faithful to her. Those separations from his child were torturous for him, so he always ended up taking her back. The final straw was when he arrived home early from his job one evening to find his wife and her mother going through his desk, presumably in an attempt to catch him cheating. He moved out that night and filed for divorce the next day.

Then he met Laine. He said he remembered her from high school, and that she was always nice to him from the first day. Mitch had moved to Bon Dieu Falls his junior year to live with his grandparents. His mom and dad were going through their own bitter and volatile divorce and had shipped him to Louisiana from Texas to weather the storm. In the end, this had been a contributing factor in his decision to stay married. He said his parents' divorce was like watching two savage animals devour each other. I could tell that it had left quite a mark on him.

Mitch said he'd known in an instant that Laine and his ex-wife were polar opposites, and he was drawn to Laine even before they'd spoken at college. He told us about watching her in the student union with a group of people, and that she was always smiling and pleasant and always helping somebody else. After several days of becoming what he described as a "creepy stalker," he got the courage to talk to her. He told us that day had completely changed his perspective about life, and he knew he'd found the woman he wanted to spend his life with. In the end, though, with his ex-wife threatening to poison his son against him, move to Canada, and keep the boy from him, he chose to go back.

I knew listening to him talk that day that he was reliving all the hurt, frustration, pain his decision had caused. Nobody could fake that kind of anguish in just telling a story. He said that Laine as usual had been most gracious about it and assured him he was doing the right thing. She said if they were meant to be together that one day they would be. He had left her apartment that day, sat in his car in the parking lot, and cried for an hour before he went home to his wife and child. Walking away from Laine remained, up until now, the hardest thing he had ever done. He was filled with regret, sadness, and guilt. But the one thing I never detected and the one thing that surprised me the most was that Mitch had no anger. That was no doubt Laine's influence.

On the fifth day after Mitch's arrival, Debra told Ella Rae and me that Laine wanted to see us. We were in the kitchen eating breakfast, and it was barely seven a.m. Laine was still in bed, so Ella Rae and I went to her bedroom and sat on either side of her bed in the big leather recliners Jack had moved in.

"Not feeling too good this morning?" I asked.

"Not so much," she said, her voice barely above a whisper.

It was the first time she ever acknowledged that, and I looked over at Ella Rae. The statement wasn't lost on her either.

"What can we do?" I asked.

"Mitch is packing," she said. "I've asked him to leave."

"Why?" Ella Rae asked, surprised. "Why would you do that? Don't you want to spend …"

"Whatever time I have left with him?" Laine asked. "No, I don't. I don't want him to see the rest of this." She gestured around the room. "The end of this."

"But he wants to be here," Ella Rae said.

"No," Laine said. "That's enough. I can't let him watch. It'll hurt him too much." She struggled a bit for another breath before she continued. "It doesn't matter how much time we have or didn't have. Never did."

I didn't understand her logic behind that, but it wasn't the first time I didn't understand the way Laine thought. But I didn't want her to waste any more energy. It was clear that every sentence was a battle.

"Stop talking, Laine," I said. "It's okay if you want him to go. Ella Rae just wanted to be sure." Laine's eyes were closed. I looked at Ella Rae and put my finger over my lips so she wouldn't ask her anything else.

"I need to say this," Laine said, struggling. "I want you to hear this. Mitch was the only man I ever loved and the only man I ever slept with. When he left me seven years ago, the last thing he said to me was 'I love you, and I'll see you again. I promise.' He said it to me again this morning." She paused, catching her breath, which was harder this time.

"Laine, you don't have to explain it," I told her. "Please stop talking. It's too hard for you. Save your strength."

She smiled a little but still didn't open her eyes. She hadn't opened them since we'd been in the room. "Save it for what, Carri? The next time Mitch sees me ... I'll be whole again ... and not like this. Maybe we didn't have the perfect love story ... but we had the perfect love 'cause it endured and it remembered and it forgave." She paused again. "Not everybody gets a gift like that. God has been so good to me, and I am so thankful." Her voice broke and tears escaped from her closed eyes.

"It *was* a beautiful love story," I said, the tears streaming down my face too. "Please don't talk anymore, Laine. Okay?"

She smiled slightly and nodded. "I love you both, you know. Stay while I sleep?"

"We love you too," I said. "Of course we'll stay."

Ella Rae couldn't answer.

Debra had given Laine a pretty strong shot for pain, and I could tell it was already working. A few minutes later, she was asleep. I adjusted the tubes of oxygen in her nose and sighed heavily.

"This ain't good, Carrigan," Ella Rae said.

"I know." For the last couple days, every time Laine went to sleep, I was afraid she wouldn't wake up. But that morning, I was horrified.

"We can't leave her today," Ella Rae said, reaching for a tissue. "At all."

"I know," I said again. I took my cell phone from my pocket and texted Jack, asking him to come to the bedroom. He was beside me in an instant.

"Hey, baby," he said softly and knelt by my chair. "What can I do?"

I bit my lip, my emotions threatening to spin out of control. "Will you go pick up Mrs. Jeanette? She ... needs to be here right now, I think. I know she and Laine have spoken about this ... but I really think she needs ... and she doesn't need to drive herself—"

"I'll go right now." He kissed my cheek. "Are you alright?"

"Probably not," I answered truthfully.

"I'll be right back," he promised. "I love you." He looked at Laine for a moment and turned to leave.

I looked at Ella Rae, whose face was ashen and frightened. "Is this the day?" she asked quietly.

"I don't know," I whispered.

I felt an uncomfortable pressure in my chest, like the one I had the day at the hospital when Dr. Rougeau was telling us Laine was going to die. I tugged the collar of my t-shirt away from my neck and tried to breathe steadily. I couldn't afford the luxury of a panic attack right now. I had to be here. I had to stay here. I had promised Laine that I wouldn't leave her, no matter what.

Debra come back into the room and put her hand on my shoulder, startling me. "I'm sorry," she said.

"What's happening here, Debra?" I asked, afraid of the answer but needing to know the truth.

Debra sighed. "No one can predict—"

"Please don't bullshit me," I said.

She nodded. "I put a catheter in last night, and there's not much output. Her blood pressure is dropping, and her color isn't good."

"And all that means?" Ella Rae asked.

"All that means ... that she's getting close to letting go," Debra said.

Neither of us replied, but we both waited for her to answer the unspoken question.

Debra pursed her lips and squeezed my shoulder. "Hours ... maybe a day at the most. I could be wrong, but ..."

Ella Rae began to cry quietly, and I felt the anger I knew so well in the pit of my stomach.

"I'm so sorry," Debra said. "I'll be right outside. If she's in pain when she wakes up, let me know."

Ella Rae and I sat on either side of Laine for the next half hour, each of us holding her hand and watching her until Mrs. Jeanette arrived. Jack brought her into the room, and I stood up to give her my chair. She hugged me tight. "Thank you for sending Jack," she said.

"He was glad to come," I said, patting her back.

She looked at Laine and tightly squeezed my hand.

"It's so hard," She said.

"I know," I told her. "Would you like for me to stay?"

"No, sweetheart. I know this is the end." Her voice broke. "And I know what she wants." She took my seat, reached for Laine's hand, and said, "Good morning, baby."

Laine moved her legs a bit and softly said, "Hey, Mama."

I motioned for Ella Rae, caught Jack's hand, and then we left Mrs. Jeanette alone to tell her daughter good-bye.

During the Christmas holidays, Laine had spoken to Mrs. Jeanette, Michael, Ella Rae, and me regarding her wishes when this time came. She had listed very few specifics, but one thing she'd been adamant about—she did *not* want her mother to watch her die. Mrs. Jeanette had been alone with Laine's father when he'd suffered the heart attack that killed him, and Laine didn't want her to watch that happen to someone else she loved. She wanted Ella Rae and me with her because "they can handle it even if they think they can't" and "it'll be easier on me, Mama, if I know you don't have to see it." Ella Rae and I hadn't spoken a word during that discussion. I knew how her request would be received, and I was right. Mrs. Jeanette balked at the idea immediately, but after Laine got pretty emotional about it, she finally relented. Laine assured her that every word they wanted or needed to say would be said before she left this earth. I was pretty sure they'd both kept that promise.

Time seemed to stand still that day. Every hour felt like it packed ninety minutes into it instead of sixty. Everybody and everything moved in super slow motion. Word gets around quickly in a small town, and people were in and out of the house all day long. Tommy and his family, the pastor at our church, and a couple of Laine's coworkers she'd been close to came to say good-bye to her. Others had come to sit with Mrs. Jeanette and offer their support or anything else we needed. Small towns ...

It started to rain around five p.m., strong thunderstorms that brought pounding showers and high winds. I looked across Laine's bed at Ella Rae after the first loud clap of thunder. Laine had always loved thunderstorms. Ella Rae smiled. I wished Laine were awake to hear this one. But she'd slept most of the day. She'd spoken to her mother for about an hour and then to Michael a few minutes after that. But since then, she'd been asleep except for a few times when she opened her eyes, looked at me and then at Ella Rae, and then closed them again.

I became increasingly anxious as the day wore on. By seven p.m., the almost constant rolling thunder was grinding on my nerves and any other sound in the house nearly made me jump out of my skin. I wanted to punch out the glass of the grandfather clock in the corner of Laine's room that grew louder and louder with each tick. I'd asked Jack to go to my parents' house an hour earlier to check on Elle, and he still wasn't back. I was worried about him driving in this weather, worried about my baby, although I knew she was in excellent hands, and worried about Ella Rae whose tears had never stopped flowing. It seemed I was back to square one, with no tears left to cry. I felt defeated and powerless. I wanted to stomp the floor, throw things, and slam doors. I knew that was stupid and childish, but I felt stupid and childish.

All my life, I had defined things by competition. It was the only way I knew how to measure anything. If you couldn't do something like dribble behind your back, lay down a perfect bunt, or outmaneuver a chick trying to take your man, you just hammered and hammered and hammered until you got it right. But I had no control over this situation with Laine. I'd never had any control over it. She'd orchestrated everything about her death right down to this minute. This was the first time in my life there was literally nothing left to do except sit by this bed and wait for her to die.

I twisted the collar away from my shirt. It was hot in here, hot enough that I was sweating, although Ella Rae had a light sweater on. Every time I looked at Laine, it seemed like her color was worse, a strange gray that no human ever needed to be. I didn't want to look at her again; in fact, I wanted to run out of this room and down the road and back to a time when my hardest decision of the day was which pair of jeans made my ass look better. I wanted my life to be fun again, and I wanted this awful, horrible nightmare to end. The thought made me so ashamed of myself, and I buried my face in my hands. How could I be wishing anything for myself while Laine was lying in bed with oxygen tubes crammed up her nose, an IV shoved in her arm, and her skin a pasty grayish-white? She was dying! And *I* felt anxious? I hated myself at that moment and wanted to claw off my own skin. Laine loved me, and I didn't deserve that. I was selfish and hateful and mean. I didn't deserve any of the things that had fallen in my lap, not Jack and not the baby. And my baby certainly didn't deserve me.

I stood up, suddenly unable to stay in this death room another second. I knew I was failing Laine, but I couldn't help it. Besides, I always failed everybody.

"Carrigan, you can't leave!" Ella Rae said.

"I … I'll be right back," I said. "I just have to … I'm gonna … I'll be back."

"Carrigan, you can't go too far."

"I *know*!" I snapped. "I said I'd be back!"

Her brows creased in question, but she didn't answer. Instead, she tucked Laine's hand back into hers and laid down on the recliner.

I slipped quickly out the bedroom door and past Debra, sitting in her ever-present chair doing cross-stitch or needlepoint or some such shit. Her eyes met mine briefly, but I didn't hang around long enough to talk. God, what a depressing life. Always living in somebody else's tragedy. I could feel her eyes on me as I picked up speed, but I didn't care. I ran into the living room where Tommy was asleep on the sofa. Dear God, was there not a place where I could be alone? I ran out the front door and right into Jack's chest.

He grabbed me by the shoulders. "Carrigan, what is it?" he asked. "Laine?"

"No," I said, pulling away from him. "She's breathing … dying … then breathing. I can't stay here." I backed away from him off the porch.

He took a step toward me.

"Don't!" I shouted. "Stay away from me!" I ran toward the barn as lightning filled the sky and the rain stung me everywhere it touched.

"Carrigan!" he shouted. "What are you doing?"

I ran in one direction and then the other to bypass his reach, but he caught me when I flung the barn door open.

"Carrigan!" he shouted again. "What's the matter?"

I backed away from him. "Did you just ask me 'what's the matter?' Are you serious?"

"I mean, what happened?" He didn't attempt to touch me this time.

I spun around so I didn't have to look at him. I was so ashamed of the things I had been thinking, of what I was still thinking. I was sure he could read them all over my face if he looked at me.

"Tell me," he shouted over the rain pounding the tin roof.

I shook my head. "I can't."

"Yes, you can," he prodded.

"I was just sitting there … waiting … just waiting, and I started thinking … I can't …" I shook my head and squeezed my eyes shut.

"Carrigan," he said, laying his hand on my shoulder from behind. "This is me you're talking to."

That sentence broke the dam. I began to cry and sobbed like I did in the rose garden the day Dr. Rougeau told us Laine was going to die, and that we'd better get used to it because we couldn't stop it, thank you very much. I cried from the pit of my soul. When I caught my breath, I bawled, yelled, and roared everything I had kept trapped inside for the past year. The words tumbled out of me on top of each other, sometimes coherent, sometimes not.

"I'm so mad at her!" I shouted and yet marveled at how good it felt to say that. "Why didn't she just take the fucking treatment? Maybe it would've made a difference! She didn't know! Was she just too chickenshit to try? She just quit! Who just quits?" I pranced around the barn, kicking dirt and throwing whatever I could get my hands on. "She just didn't even *try!* It makes no sense! Her God gives out miracles very day! Surely He would've given her one. Surely! But no. She just laid there." I gestured to the house. "She just laid there and withered and withered and withered, and now she's gonna die!" I kicked a water bucket and scared the horses. "Nobody just quits! I can't even …" I plopped down on a bale of hay, put my hands over my face, and then jerked them away again.

Jack moved toward me, but I put my hand out to stop him. "No," I said. "No, there's more. Don't touch me. Did you hear all the shit I just said? About my best friend? The one who is dying while I am out here screaming about how pissed off I am? How selfish is that? Who does that, Jack?" I felt another wave of self-loathing spill over me. "I am an awful, horrible person. I don't deserve her! I don't deserve you! And Elle?" I shrieked. "She *surely* doesn't deserve me! I'm not fit to be a mother! A cow's a better mother than I am! Would you want me to be your mother? Of course not! A mother is supposed to be stable! I feel crazy! Crazy!!"

I jumped up again to throw something, but this time Jack caught me in his arms and held me there. After I twisted and turned, trying to remove myself from his grip, it became evident that he wasn't going to let me, so I stopped fighting, slumped against him, and began to cry again.

"Just get it out," Jack said and held me against him while I wept into his chest.

I was so exhausted I wanted to just let myself go limp in his arms, but I knew I couldn't. "I'm sorry," I mumbled into his shirt.

"Sorry for what?" he asked.

"For everything," I said. I felt too guilty to even look at him.

He pushed me away from him gently and curled his finger under my chin. "I'm gonna tell you something," he said. "And I want you to listen to me very carefully, okay?"

I nodded.

Jack cradled my face in his hands and said, "I don't know another person who loves people any deeper than you do. So I don't wanna hear what a bad person you are. You are the mother of my child, and I wouldn't want anybody else on earth to have that job. And I hope she turns out just like you. Full of grit and spirit and life."

He sat on a bale of hay and pulled me down onto his lap. "I wish Laine would've tried the treatment too. But, Carri, it doesn't matter how I feel or how you feel. She's the one in that bed. You can't want something *for* somebody. You forget that she doesn't have the will or the fight in her that you have. She can't pick up that pitchfork and take on the world. Not five years ago or ten years ago. And you can't expect her to now."

I didn't answer him, but I knew he was right. Laine wasn't a fighter in any sense of the word. Laine was a peacemaker. Always had been.

"Besides," he said, "you aren't really mad at her about the chemo. You're mad at her for dying."

That had punched me in the gut. "But that's not her fault," I said.

"Exactly," he answered.

I let that sink in a moment. How could you be mad at someone for dying? Laine couldn't help it. She'd done nothing to give herself cancer. The truth was, the harsh and high dosage of chemotherapy needed to treat her cancer would have made her a lot sicker a lot faster. Laine wasn't physically strong. She never had been. I didn't really blame her for not taking it. Jack was right. I was mad at her because she was leaving me. Not on a little vacation or a week on the beach. She wasn't coming back. Ever. She was such a huge, important part of my life, and her absence would leave a hole impossible to fill.

How would Ella Rae and I live without our other piece? The puzzle would be forever broken. We were going to Ireland one day. We were going to Hawaii one day. We were supposed to build houses together and have babies together and have lives together. She was supposed to be here for those things, and now we had to do them without her. How dare she just walk off in the fourth inning? What would Ella Rae and I ever do without her? How do you let go of somebody you love so much?

I sighed heavily and felt the anger drain out of me. I wasn't selfish after all. I was grieving. And there was no right way to do it.

Jack tugged on my thick braid. "You're so tired, baby. I'm surprised this didn't happen sooner."

I relaxed against him. Just his presence calmed me, but his words tonight had cured me. The heaviness I had carried inside for so long felt different now, lighter. I'd become so accustomed to it that I barely noticed it anymore. The anger had become as much a part of me as my arms and legs. Maybe it would never go away entirely, but tonight, I even felt physically lighter. I felt my spirit filling up like water pouring into a reservoir. I held him close to me. "You are such a good man, and I love you."

"You are a remarkable woman, and I love you too," Jack said.

I took his hand, and we headed toward the door. I could help her do this now. I could help her finish it.

Chapter 16

"*A*re you alright?" Ella Rae asked when I got back to Laine's room.

"I'm fine," I answered. "How is she?"

Ella Rae shook her head. "Not sleeping well."

I got into my recliner and reached for Laine's hand.

"Move over," Jack said.

"Jack, you are going to be so uncomfortable, you don't have to—"

"I've been uncomfortable before," he said.

I moved over in the chair, and Jack eased his over six-foot frame down behind me. I was grateful he was here. I looked at Laine, and my heart softened. I wasn't mad at her anymore. I couldn't believe I ever had been. Of course she would never leave us if she had a choice. She'd gone along with every stupid idea I ever had. She'd compromised her standards a thousand times to accommodate my lack of them. She'd fought for my marriage when I hadn't. She pushed and pulled and pleaded with Ella Rae and me to be better people. She'd had my back so many times that I couldn't remember them all, and now she was leaving me. She loved me, and I was losing her, and that was what I had been mad about all along. I still had no idea how it would feel when she was gone, but I felt an unfamiliar yet welcome peace begin to surround me. I closed my eyes and let it wash over me. What sweet relief to put an end to the constant turmoil that had boiled inside me for the past year. I pulled Jack's arm closer around me and held Laine's hand a little tighter.

"Close your eyes, and try to rest," Jack whispered.

I squeezed his hand but didn't answer. I brushed a stand of hair away from Laine's face and smiled. She'd been so happy the past few days while Mitch was here. I had never seen her act the way she did when he was around. She was clearly and absolutely in love with him. I still couldn't believe she'd never told us about him or that we'd never picked up on it. Guys asked her out all the time. Sometimes she would go. But after a couple of dates, she never went out with them again. Ella Rae and I said her standards were too high, and she said we had none. But never once did I think her lack of dating had anything to do with a love affair that never really ended for either of them. A love affair so fierce and consuming that everything else paled in comparison. A perfect love indeed.

But the last five days had a different effect on Mitch. I walked him to his car when he left that morning and held him while he cried. Those deep, gut-wrenching sobs that echo anguish in your own heart. He apologized to me for a while and then thanked me for a while. My heart ached for him all day. What a terrible situation this was for him. Trapped in a loveless marriage, trying to do the right thing, and when he finally becomes free, he finds the love of his life like this. Any animosity I'd had for him had completely disappeared. He was just as hurt as Ella Rae and I, and probably even more so, as his pain was laced with regret and guilt. He begged me to persuade Laine to let him stay. I told him I would try, but I knew it was futile. Laine had made up her mind, and as we'd all learned in the last few months, once she decided on a course of action, she didn't change it. I liked Mitch Montgomery and was sorry to see him drive away.

Jack was right. I was mentally, physically, and emotionally exhausted. Still, sleep wouldn't come. I laid my head on the cool leather of the recliner and watched Laine sleep. I thought about grammar school and how Ella Rae was forever beating the crap out of somebody who picked on Laine. I thought about junior high and high school, our first real dates, which we'd all gone on together. I thought about summer camps, football games, bike rides, shopping trips, and proms. I almost laughed out loud as I remembered the weekend Jack and I got married and Laine had spent the entire three days in a panic because she was worried about the fallout. I thought about the nights, not so long ago, we rode around all night long, listening to music and drinking beer. Laine would sip water and preach the whole night about how pointless it was to ride around while we could sit in a house and listen to a new CD. It was safer, she argued. It was boring, we said. She rolled her eyes and complained, told us we were killing her, as she never got any rest and wanted to go home. She reminded us that she was the only one with a real job and needed real sleep. But the truth is, bamboo under her fingernails couldn't have made her exit that vehicle with us still in it. I thought about the night in Shreveport when she was sneaking around the parking lot like a cat, ready to pounce at the slightest sound. The girl wouldn't step on a spider but would fight a grizzly bear for me. We'd lived so much, but I wanted so much more.

I must've fallen asleep at some point because I woke with a start, like something had jerked me awake. I glanced at the clock. It was 2:12 a.m. Ella Rae was asleep, still holding Laine's hand. Jack was asleep beside me. In fact, the only sound at all was the steady hum of Laine's oxygen and the grandfather clock. I looked at Laine. She was awake and smiling at me, very slightly, but she was smiling. She stared into my eyes so intently that I realized she must've willed me awake.

"Hey," I whispered. "Do you need anything?"

She didn't nod or answer. She just kept looking at me with that faint, faraway smile. I laid my head back down and stayed locked in her gaze. When I think back on that moment, I am sure I saw a multitude of emotions in her eyes—peace, gratitude, love, even joy. Then she took a deep breath, exhaled, and then didn't breathe again. I stared at her chest, waiting for the rise and fall that never came. Just like that, Laine was gone.

A low "oh" came from my lips, but I didn't move. She'd slipped out of this world and into the next without crash carts, bells and whistles, or white coats. Just like she wanted. I was grateful for that, even as hot tears poured down my face. I held her hand against my cheek for a minute or maybe an hour, I still don't know. I never wanted to move from that chair. As long Laine was in that bed, we could still see her, talk to her, touch her … even if she was dying. But I knew when I woke the others, her life would truly be over, and I still wanted it to be our secret. I whispered, "I love you" over and over again during that treasured time I shared with her.

Finally, I knew that her spirit was gone. I felt it as sure as I could feel the sun on my face or the wind in my hair. Laine wasn't here anymore. Reluctantly, I laid her hand gently across her chest and sat up.

"Ella Rae," I said. "Ella Rae."

She bolted upright in her chair, Laine's hand still tucked in her own. She knew as soon as she looked at me. Even though she hadn't yet looked at Laine, she knew it just the same and began to cry. "I wasn't ready," she said. "I wasn't ready yet."

Jack stood up and pulled me close to him. "I'm so sorry," he said, kissing the top of my head.

I nodded against his chest, my tears still falling, but I wasn't frantic like I had imagined I would be when this moment came. I still felt the peace that had wrapped itself around me earlier, even more so now after she'd gone. She hadn't struggled or fought or resisted. She just … didn't breathe again. In many ways, I was feeling huge relief, like someone had removed a ton of bricks from my shoulders. I had been amazed by her life and was now amazed by her death. "Please get Tommy, Jack," I said.

Ella Rae was struggling. I moved out of Jack's arms and held her close to me. She was inconsolable. "I knew she was going to die, but I wasn't ready! I didn't want her to die!"

Ella Rae laid her head on Laine's chest and sobbed. I placed my hand on her back, helpless to do much else, and let her cry. Sweet Rae. Ready to defend either of us at the drop of a hat, a tiny little thing that would take on anybody who threatened Laine or me. But if she loved you, she was gentle as a lamb.

Tommy came in quickly and took Ella Rae into his arms. "It's okay, baby," he soothed. "It's gonna be okay."

"I wasn't ready," she said again and again. "I didn't want her to die."

Tommy, in his Southern boy logic that I had always loved and admired, told her, "It don't matter what you wanted, baby. This world didn't want her anymore. Shhh … baby, it's gonna be okay."

Debra came in and removed the oxygen tubes from Laine's nose and gently took the IV from her hand. She folded Laine's hands in her lap and started to pull the sheet over her.

"Wait!" I said. Although I was calm and the peaceful feeling remained, I wasn't ready for that. "Please, can you just not do that yet?"

Debra stepped away from the bed. "Of course," she said and turned to leave the room. When she got to the doorway, she stopped and looked at us. "I have had the privilege of working with many families," she said. "But I have never seen the amount of love and support among people who weren't blood relatives as I've seen here. It's been an honor, and I am so sorry for your loss. She was a treasure." She closed the door gently behind her.

Jack leaned over the bed and kissed Laine on her forehead. "Good-bye, sweet girl," he said with tears in his eyes and then patted her hand. My heart broke. I knew how much Jack loved and respected her, and Laine had adored him. She believed in us when we didn't believe in ourselves.

Ella Rae calmed down somewhat, and I put my arms around her. I knew a multitude of people loved Laine, but nobody else felt exactly the same way I did except Ella Rae. We held each other for a long time and cried without saying a word. Then we stood by Laine's bedside for the last time. Finally, I pulled Ella Rae away and said, "Come on, Rae. We have a celebration to plan."

Chapter 17

"What the hell?" I gasped as the funeral director walked out of the room to let us view Laine's body alone.

"Oh shit!" Ella Rae said.

"She looks like a hooker!"

"Oh shit!" Ella Rae said, louder this time.

"Shut up, Rae! He's gonna hear you!"

"He needs to hear me! Who's the makeup artist around here? The bouncer at Sugar and Spice? That is ho-red lipstick!"

"Keep your voice down, and give me something!" I said.

"Like what? A washtub and some bleach?"

"Jesus, Ella Rae. Just reach in your suit-purse, and get me something! Mrs. Jeanette and Michael will be here any minute!"

She pulled out a toothbrush.

"Really?" I asked.

She dug some more and came up with makeup remover wipes.

"Thank God!" I said and began scrubbing Laine's lips. "Help me!"

She wiped at the bright-blue eye shadow. "What is this shit? All-weather stain?"

"There!" I said, effectively removing the red paint. I reached into my purse and pulled out my coral lipstick and carefully applied it to Laine's lips—until Ella Rae's elbow bumped my hand and I dropped it, that is, leaving a thin coral line down the front of Laine's pale-pink dress. "Dammit, Ella Rae!"

"'Dammit, Ella Rae'? You're the one who dropped it!"

"Give me something!" I said.

She pulled out a laundry stick.

I stared at her. "You keep a laundry stick in your purse?"

"What's wrong with that?" she said, indignant.

"Nothing's *wrong* with it," I answered, shrugging my shoulders. "It's just something my grandmother would do."

She put a hand on her hip. "At least I don't put maxi pads on my titties."

"They are *NOT*—. Oh, never mind. Just help me!"

Finally, we got the stain out of Laine's dress, applied a subtle light-brown shadow on her lids, and covered her lips in coral. She looked like Laine again. Then we really looked at her. She looked peaceful, just like she was asleep. But this mahogany box with its ornate handles and satin pillow held the truth inside it. Our friend wasn't asleep; she was gone. She wasn't coming back. It was over. I clasped Ella Rae's hand. She was crying, of course, but my tears had dried up. I dreaded the next two days, yet at the same time, I wished they'd go on and on. At least we would celebrate Laine's life at the wake and the funeral. But when we went home, it would all be over, and I knew that's when the real battle would begin.

Laine had been adamant about our closing her casket. She only wanted four people to see her in this coffin—Ella Rae, Mrs. Jeanette, Michael, and me. But he'd only consented to that because she knew we'd need to see her, to tell her good-bye. She wanted people to remember her as she was, not "all dressed up and sleeping in a box," as she put it. When the lid closed on this casket, it wouldn't be opened again. That realization made me anxious.

I'd been so calm since Laine had passed. Serene, almost. I was still in awe about watching her leave this world, how gentle and comforting it had been. But now, looking at her, it became all too real. A slight panic or at least a heightened awareness started to sink in. Laine *died*. *She died*. There would be a wake and then a funeral, and we would *bury* her. We'd all go home, but Laine would stay at the cemetery. And somewhere between all of that, I had to stand up in church, in front of everybody I knew, and explain to them who Laine Elizabeth Landry was. How could I do that? I wasn't at all worried about speaking in front of people, but I was horrified at summing up Laine's life in twenty minutes. How could I ever make these people understand who she really was? I had *lived* who she was. Ella Rae had lived who she was. I couldn't do her life justice by telling someone about it. For weeks, I had attempted to put something on paper for this occasion, but nothing ever sounded right. So the day before I was to deliver her eulogy, I still had no idea what I was going to say.

"Mrs. Jeanette and Michael are here," Ella Rae whispered.

I leaned over and kissed Laine's cheek, and Ella Rae followed suit.

"You'll always be with us," I whispered to her.

"Always," Ella Rae promised.

We walked away and met Mrs. Jeanette and Michael at the entrance of the room.

"Does my baby look pretty?" Mrs. Jeanette asked, her voice broken and small.

"She does," I promised.

She hugged Ella Rae and me tightly. "I will never be able to thank you girls enough for what you did," she cried. "And Carrigan, Jack and the Whitfield's ... how can I ever repay—?"

"There's no need for that," I told her. "They were happy to do it, and Laine would've done it for any of us. You know that."

She shook her head. "They just went above and beyond, and I am eternally grateful."

"They loved her," I said and glanced back at the coffin. "Everybody did."

"Yes, they did," she said. "We'll see you at the church."

Ella Rae and I hugged Michael and left the room so they could be alone with Laine.

Two hours later, Ella Rae and I sat outside our church in the back parking lot and waited for the wake to begin. They had brought Laine's body from the funeral home and were setting up the casket inside the church. We watched somberly as they'd wheeled it in the door in the misty rain. The weather report had called for rain the rest of the week. *Great, so the proverbial black cloud really does exist*, I thought.

Even though the wake didn't officially start until five p.m., people had already started streaming into the fellowship hall, bringing food. That was a huge Southern tradition. I didn't know how they did things in the rest of the country, but in the South when somebody died, you cooked all day. I watched them trail in, one after the other, and knew that somewhere in all those containers lurked pecan pies, fried chicken, rice and gravy, cornbread, every fresh vegetable imaginable, and a whole lot of sweet tea. I also knew Mrs. Birdie Jordan would show up with a hummingbird cake that tasted like a thick honey bun. She had to be about 130 years old by now, but she could still bang out a cake. My stomach rumbled just thinking about it. I couldn't remember when I'd last eaten a full meal. I had gone to my parent's house that morning to nurse Elle and leave more bottles and grabbed a piece of toast. At least, I thought it had been that morning. My days had tumbled on top of each other.

Mrs. Jeanette had asked Ella Rae and me to stand in the receiving line with her and Michael. That was also known as stand beside the coffin and say "thank you for coming" all night. But I was grateful for that. I didn't want to miss seeing a single person who came to tell Laine good-bye.

Mitch drove up as we were walking in the back door of the church, and we waited for him under the porch. He'd been at the farm since early that morning. Ella Rae and I had spoken with him earlier, and he seemed to be doing pretty well. Mrs. Jeanette had asked him to stand with us tonight, but he'd declined. I think he felt it would somehow take the attention off Laine if everyone wondered who he was and why he was there. But we made him promise to come early, and he had complied. The three of us walked into the back door of the church.

"Mrs. Whitfield?" a voice said.

I looked around for Jack's mother.

"He's talking to you, stupid!" Ella Rae said.

"Oh! Yes, I'm Mrs. Whitfield." If I lived to be a hundred, I'd never get used to that.

"Mrs. Landry asked that you all join her in the front of the church," the funeral director told me.

"Thank you," I said and walked toward the sanctuary.

"He was creepy," Ella Rae said.

"No, he wasn't," I said.

"Whatever," Ella Rae retorted.

Jack was placing Laine's picture that we had enlarged and framed on the table beside the casket. It was stunning. We'd chosen an antique gold frame that complemented the colors in the picture beautifully. She looked amazing in the photograph—happy, healthy, and full of life, just what I wanted. Everyone thought it was perfect. Ella Rae and I were going to give it to Mrs. Jeanette after the services.

"Mrs. Landry," the voice behind us said as we admired Laine's picture. "It's five o'clock. Time to open the doors."

Ella Rae looked at me with wide eyes as the funeral director walked away. "How does he just appear like that?" she whispered. "Creepy!"

I shook my head and smiled. It would be a long night in more ways than one. "Come on." I took her hand. "Let's get in our places."

We stood beside Mrs. Jeanette and Michael and waited for the doors to open so our town could pay their respects and say good-bye to Laine. I looked at the front pew and touched Ella Rae's arm. "Look," I said.

Jack, Tommy, and Mitch were sitting together. We both smiled. All our handsome men were on the front pew of the First Baptist Church of Bon Dieu Falls. Laine would've been ecstatic.

From the moment the doors opened at five o'clock until ten, we greeted, spoke to, and thanked people. Everyone had a story they wanted to share or a memory they passed along to us. I was amazed at the number of people who had shown up and even more so at the things they had to say. They told us things about Laine we had never known. Mrs. Leta Gray, an elderly woman who lived in town, said Laine had picked up her prescription at the pharmacy every month before she'd gotten sick and then called to apologize because she couldn't do it anymore. Mrs. Jessie Rodgers told us how she had feared she'd have to give up her beloved rat terrier because her social security check had been cut, and she couldn't afford to keep him anymore. Laine heard her granddaughter talking about it at school, so every Friday evening after that, Laine brought her a sack of dog food. When she got sick, she left instructions at the bank to give Mrs. Jesse twenty dollars every Friday. Laine had bought basketball shoes for Kristie Williams's son, a Halloween costume for another child, and an Easter basket for another child. The list went on and on. Ella Rae and I were stunned. Laine had never said a word about any of it. Those stories remain some of my most cherished memories of her. I truly understood that night how comforting words can be.

By ten p.m., I was almost too exhausted to stand. My breasts ached, my feet hurt, and my stomach was growling loud enough for everybody in the place to hear it. Jack had come around three different times to ask Ella Rae and me to go to the fellowship hall to eat, but we didn't want to leave. But once the line dwindled, I was about to excuse myself to Mrs. Jeanette when Ella Rae said, "Twelve o'clock."

I looked down the aisle and saw Lexi Carter moving toward us. For a moment, a tug of long-forgotten angst stirred inside me, but only fleetingly. She looked old and worn and tired. For some reason, I immediately felt sorry for her, and I had no idea where that had come from. She walked up to us and offered her hand. "When I heard about Laine, I had to come pay my respects," she said sincerely, looking at Ella Rae and then at me. "She was a really good person ... and I wanted to tell you ... I am sorry ... about many things. I didn't mean to ... Well ... I'm sorry."

I took her hand. "Thank you for coming, Lexi." And I meant it. "And thank you for your kind words." I thought for a moment and then added, "You should say hello to Jack before you go."

She smiled. "I will, Carrigan," she said. "And congratulations on the new baby. I know you'll be great parents." She spotted Jack and said, "I'll just go say hello. And I really am so sorry about Laine."

Ella Rae had watched it all without opening her mouth. I was more shocked about that than I was about Lexi Carter making an appearance.

"What the hell just happened?" Ella Rae asked.

"Shut up, Rae," I said. "You can't curse in church."

"Like God can't hear me when I'm outside? Why did you just send Lexi to see Jack? And by the way, he is freaking out. Look at him!"

Poor Jack. He looked very uncomfortable. He glanced up at me, and I smiled at him and nodded. "It's okay," I mouthed.

"You are a better woman than I am," Ella Rae said.

"She's kinda pitiful," I said. "I mean, look at her. And I'm *not* trying to be funny here … she looks rode hard and put up wet." I shook my head. "Life hasn't been good to her."

"That's called karma, Carri," Ella Rae said.

I shrugged. "Whatever it is, it doesn't matter."

Jack slid his arm around my waist and kissed the top of my head. "You need to eat," he said.

Tommy joined us, and we excused ourselves with Mrs. Jeanette, who thanked us profusely for helping her receive guests.

When we got outside, I stopped at the door of the fellowship hall. "I can't talk to another person tonight," I told Jack. "I just can't." I was so tired that I felt numb. At some point during the evening, my tear ducts started working again, and my emotions were running rampant. I was crying, I was laughing, I was fine, and then I was crying and then laughing and then fine again.

"I can't either," Ella Rae said.

Jack ushered us around to the side of the fellowship hall where there was a fountain and some benches. "Sit," he said. "We'll be right back."

He didn't get an argument from either of us, and we waited in silence. A few minutes later, Jack and Tommy showed up with four plates of food and a gallon of tea.

"We didn't know what you wanted, so we got a little bit of all of it," Tommy said and gave us two plastic forks.

Ella Rae and I dug in like we'd been starving in the desert, sharing plates and drinking out of the pitcher. The food was delicious, just like I knew it would be. The hummingbird cake was even better than I remembered.

I hadn't realized Jack and Tommy were watching us until Tommy said, "Y'all eat like men."

"What do you mean?" Ella Rae asked and then took a gulp out of the jug of tea.

"That's what I mean!" .

"Do you see a glass?"

"We would've gotten you some," Tommy answered.

"No need," I told him and took a gulp myself.

"No use, Tommy," Jack said, shaking his head. "They have their own language. Always have."

Twenty minutes later, we were both so stuffed we could hardly move. It was getting close to midnight, and the crowd had thinned considerably. Mrs. Jeanette and Michael had just left, and I knew we'd soon be the only ones left in the sanctuary. People would stay in the fellowship hall all night because that's just what we did in Bon Dieu Falls. But the church doors would be locked at midnight and not opened again until eight in the morning. I thought I could do it, but now I was having second thoughts. I looked at Ella Rae and knew she was thinking the same thing.

"Jack," I said. "Will you do something for us?"

"You know I will."

"Will you go over to our house and get Ella Rae and me some blankets and pillows?" I bit my lip as a new wave of tears came to town. "We can't leave her by herself, Jack. We just can't."

"We promised her we never would," Ella Rae said, whose tears never seemed to stop.

He sighed, and I knew he was about to protest. He wanted me to go home and sleep all night.

"Please," I said. "We'll never be able to do another thing for her."

"Alright. But if you stay, Tommy and I stay in the fellowship hall tonight." He looked at Tommy.

"Agreed," Tommy said.

"Okay," I said. "Just call Mama, and check on Elle. My phone is in Ella Rae's car."

"I will. We'll be right back." He and Tommy then left.

Ella Rae and I remained on the bench, too tired to talk and too emotionally spent to carry on much of a conversation anyway. We simply sat on the bench and held hands. It was such a comfort that I didn't even mind the sandpaper.

Just before midnight, we went back into the sanctuary to find Creepy Guy escorting out the last of the guests. Jack and Tommy arrived with our things and prepared a makeshift bed on either end of the center pew for us.

Jack kissed me lightly and said, "Come get us if you need anything. We'll be checking on you throughout the night. I know you needed to stay, Carri, but please try to sleep, baby. You're so tired."

"I will," I promised.

Tommy said goodnight to Ella Rae and left the sanctuary with Jack.

Ella Rae and I lay on opposite ends of the pew and stared at the mahogany box and the smiling girl in the giant picture on the easel.

"She was so pretty" Ella Rae said.

"She really was."

It was most comforting lying there, and I couldn't believe we'd ever considered going home that night. This was where we were supposed to be. One last sleepover. When I closed my eyes, I fell into a deep and dreamless sleep, more restful than I'd had in weeks.

❧ *Chapter 18* ❧

"*W*ake up, Carri." I could hear Ella Rae's voice, but I couldn't seem to open my eyes. "Wake up!"

I finally opened my eyes but had no idea where I was.

"Church," Ella Rae said, standing over me.

"Yes." I sat up.

"We need to go. And if I look as bad as you do, we need to go now."

"Am I a train wreck?"

"Except for where we are, you're kinda the poster child for the walk of shame," Ella Rae said.

I tried to smooth the wrinkles out of my black dress, but that didn't work at all. A strand of hair was wrapped around my pearls, keeping me from turning my head. And I had apparently slept on top of one of my heels because it was folded in half. I laughed in spite of the situation. After all, it was the first time I had ever spent the night on a church pew, guarding a coffin. Maybe this was the way you were supposed to look the next morning.

Ella Rae rolled up the blanket and threw the pillow on top.

"Laine wouldn't like the way you folded that blanket." I smiled.

She smiled back at me. "She was a little bit OCD, you know that, don't you?"

"You think? What gave her away? The pantry with the cans alphabetized? Or the color-coordinated closet?"

"I was thinking more like that weird thing she did with her dishes," Ella Rae answered. "You know, blue plate, green plate, yellow plate."

We laughed and looked at Laine's picture.

"Come on," Ella Rae said. "I don't wanna leave her either, but we're gonna look pretty stupid dragging her around behind us."

Shortly after, Jack and I were on the way home. Neither Jack nor Tommy had slept at all last night, and around two a.m., Mitch had joined them. Mitch had left the wake around ten and headed out to the farm but ended up driving around a couple hours and then coming back to the church. Jack said Mitch was going to have a tough time dealing with Laine's death even more than Ella Rae and I would.

"His guilt is going to eat him alive if he lets it," Jack said. "I know how that feels."

I touched his hand. "Jack, if that was about what happened between us ... really, it doesn't matter. It's over. Done."

"Pull over," he said.

"What?"

"Just pull off the road for a minute," he repeated.

I drove into the parking lot at the softball field and stopped the car.

"Look at me," Jack said.

I turned to face him, and he caught both of my hands in his.

"I am sorry, Carrigan," he said. "I know I've said it before. But last night, watching Mitch so torn up and so ... sorry ... He can never make it up to her."

I felt horrible listening to him and seeing his face contorted with guilt and pain. I tried to stop him again. "Jack, really ... it doesn't—"

"Just listen. Please. I was a fool, Carrigan," he said. "Our life together was good. It was better than good. But I let someone else inside it ... About three years ago, Lexi called me out of the blue. She called me at the farm."

Last night's goodwill for Lexi Carter disappeared inside five seconds, and I felt the anger I associated with her again. But I didn't say anything. I wanted Jack to finish this story.

"She said she was in town and wanted to say hello, wanted me to meet her for lunch, but I said no. I never loved Lexi, Carrigan. I want you to know that. I liked her, and we had fun together, but I never loved her. And she knew it."

He looked at me, waiting for me to respond. When I didn't, he continued.

"We talked a long time that day," he said. "Eventually, the subject turned to you and me. I told her things were great, and they were. I told her the truth. She said she'd heard some things about you that she thought I should know. And I know I should've cut her off then. But I didn't."

I was getting increasingly angry, but I wanted to know the rest. "Go on."

"She said a friend from Bon Dieu Falls had told her you were getting restless. In the marriage. She said you were making comments at the diner about how bored you were all day, and how you needed something more. I didn't believe her, Carrigan." He paused and looked out the window. "But I started paying better attention after that."

I don't know what kept me calm in the car that day, but a year earlier I would have clawed his eyes out just from what he'd said so far. Maybe it was because it was the day of Laine's funeral. Maybe I had matured over the course of the year. Or maybe I was just curious. But whatever it was, I didn't speak until he was finished.

"A few days after I talked to Lexie," Jack said, "I overheard a conversation you were having with Ella Rae. You said you wondered what going to college would've felt like. I heard you talk about the scholarship." He looked at me. "You'd never told me you turned down a softball scholarship. I felt like a piece of shit. I had taken all that away from you."

I felt my heart soften a little. This was exactly why I'd never told him about the scholarship. I knew he'd feel this way.

"But it wasn't just the scholarship," he said. "There were other things too. You'd stopped coming to the farm to work. You weren't happy, and I knew it. I had to let you go, but I couldn't ask you for a divorce. Not even when I thought I should have. It would've been like cutting my own arm off. I wanted you to have all that you missed. You were still young. So I thought if I … treated you badly enough, you'd ask me for one." He took my hand again. "But all I saw was how much I was hurting you. Even when you … went somewhere else for comfort." He shook his head. "It's my fault, and I'll spend the rest of our lives making it up to you."

I was stunned. Jack had known all along. But of course he did! Jack always knew everything. I didn't know what to say. "Jack, I'm so sorry!" I grabbed him and held him close to me. "I'm so sorry!" I was so ashamed of myself that I didn't want to look at him.

"It's not your fault," he said, his voice breaking. "I drove you away. And I haven't been a saint either. So stop punishing yourself."

I looked at him. He'd just told me he'd cheated on me too. I'd spent two years trying to figure it out and trying to catch him, and now he'd just admitted it. Only now I didn't care; his confession meant nothing to me. I didn't even want to know who the woman was. It was like we were talking about two completely different people, not ourselves.

I kept my head down, but he put his hands on my face and lifted it. "I love you," he said. "I didn't tell you this so you'd be upset. I hate what I did to you. But whatever you did was because of me. I wanted you to know what happened so you'd never feel guilty again. I watched a man cry last night and listened to him spill his guts to two complete strangers, and it got to me. We've made mistakes, Carrigan, but that's all they were. And we have a chance to fix ours."

"I'm so sorry," I said again. "It meant nothing to me. I swear."

"I know," he said and gathered me into his arms.

"And I didn't give a damn about playing softball in college."

"You still gave it up for me."

"I gave it up for *me*. I didn't want to be a college softball player. I'm too lazy! You know that's true! And I don't know what conversation you overheard, but it was a fleeting moment, I promise you." He started to speak. "No, it's my turn to talk! I stopped working at the farm because I was useless, Jack. You made up a job for me, not because you needed me. I didn't want Mr. Jack to have to pay me to screw things up. And maybe I wasn't happy for a while. I was … restless. But it wasn't because of you. I thought you wanted me to work, and that I had disappointed you. I may have said that crap at the diner. Who knows? But it wasn't because I didn't want to be married. All I *ever* wanted to be was your wife. That's it! And I don't ever want to talk about any of this again."

He studied my face for a minute before speaking. "I lost my faith in you. I was so sure you wanted out."

"I never wanted out," I said. "Never."

He kissed me, and he kissed me thoroughly. So thoroughly that I bit my lip when he was done. Would the man ever stop making my knees weak?

"If we're done with the confessions, can we go see our daughter now?" I asked.

He smiled. "We're done. Damn, that felt good."

"Which part, the talk or the kiss?" I smiled.

"All of it," he said. He closed his eyes and leaned back in the seat. "It's behind us. Let's leave it there."

I was relieved it was all out on the table now. No secrets, nothing to hide, ever again. Maybe I would've been more curious about who Jack had been with if I had been innocent. But I wasn't innocent. I didn't want to talk about my indiscretions, so I wasn't going to make him talk about his. It may have been Lexi, but I really didn't think so. I think her apology last night was intended for the letter she wrote long ago and for planting doubt in Jack's mind years later. I knew she was sincere then, and I still believed it. It didn't exactly endear her to me, but I no longer wanted to pull her eyes out of their sockets either. I could tell from our brief encounter at the wake that Lexi Carter was a mess. Maybe she'd gotten involved in drugs or some other excessive lifestyle, but whatever it was, Lexi wasn't the same. I felt sorry for her, even though she did try to take Jack away from me on several occasions. But I could let it go now. She didn't matter anymore. There were far more important things happening in our lives, and Jack and I were becoming closer than we'd ever been. I knew I never had to worry about the Lexi Carters of this world again.

When I saw my mother's car as soon as we got to the farm, I knew my baby was inside. I took the steps two at a time, even in my heels. Mama was holding Elle, and Mrs. Diane was showing her a new rag doll. I rushed straight to them.

"Hi, my baby!" I said and took her from my mother. Elle felt so warm and smelled so good. Just having her in my arms was like tonic for my soul. I held her little body against me as tightly as I could without breaking her. I closed my eyes and drank her in, her coos, her nuzzles, her soft baby skin that smelled like lotion and everything in the world that was sweet. Just seeing her made the world seem right again, even if it were only for a little while. I felt the tears I didn't realize were coming roll down my cheeks.

"I'm sorry," I said to my mother and Mrs. Diane. "I don't even know where they come from. You know I'm not much of a crier, at least I never was one before."

"You've never lost Laine before," my mother said, rubbing my back. "It hurts."

"How long will it feel like this?" I gave Elle to Mrs. Diane. I didn't want to hold her and sob.

"Sweetheart, there's no time limit on grief," mama told me. "It would be nice if it had an expiration date, but it doesn't. There are many days I want to pick up the phone and call your grandmother, and she's been gone for years."

I could remember times when my mother had said, "I wish I could talk to Mama today" and then go on about her day. She still grieved my grandparents. I missed them too and had been crushed when Papaw died and then again a few years later when Mamaw passed. But I had argued those last months that while death was sad for everyone, Laine's being young made it different. I had operated under the assumption that my grief was greater because Laine still had things to do in her life, but it was cut short. But it wasn't true. Perhaps Laine's age made it more tragic, but my grief was no greater than my mother's. It wasn't the person's age that made death sad; it was the absence in the lives of the ones left behind that did. My mother and grandmother were together every day. Mama felt her absence more than the rest of us, like Ella Rae and I would feel Laine's absence.

I suddenly felt sorry for my mother and hugged her tight. "I'm so sorry about Mamaw," I said.

"Oh, sweetheart," she said. "It's alright. All these things you feel are normal. That's the bad thing about grief. You have to go through it, not around it."

I cried in my mother's arms and was amazed how her voice soothed me. I realized why she missed my grandmother so much.

"Carrigan," Mrs. Diane said finally. "I hate to ask right now, but it's meal time for Elle. Do you want me to give her a bottle or would you like to do that?"

"I want to nurse her. I want to hold her before I have to get ready to ... go back."

Mrs. Diane gave Elle to me, and I took her into the nursery where we could be alone. I had missed my baby so much. Jack came into the nursery and sat on the daybed.

"Is she hungry?" he asked.

"She's starving," I said. "Like a little pig."

He watched as I nursed our daughter for a few minutes then asked, "Are we good, Carrigan?"

I smiled. "We're better than good. We're the best we've ever been."

Jack smiled that smile that never failed to make my heart beat fast, no matter the circumstances. "Yes, we are."

Chapter 19

The church was already near capacity when Jack and I arrived at noon. After last night's testaments, I don't know why that surprised me. I had thought I'd be back soon enough so Ella Rae and I could spend a few minutes alone with Laine for the last time, but Ella Rae wasn't even back yet.

Jack and I made our way through the back entrance of the church, and I headed straight to Laine's casket. Strange as it sounds, standing next to it made me feel better. I sighed and rubbed the cool, smooth mahogany. I wanted to make Creepy Guy open the coffin just so I could look at her again, but I knew that was out of the question. I briefly toyed with the idea of popping the top myself, but Laine would probably sit up and slap me. I bent down and placed my face against the cool wood. "I'm back," I whispered. "Rae's on her way."

The mahogany felt so good against my face. I stayed in that position and talked to Laine. I wasn't crying or upset. I just wanted to talk to her. I told her about how sweet Elle had been that morning, and how I wished she'd been there to see her. I told her how upset Mitch had been the night before and to send him some comfort if she found a way. I stroked the mahogany and whispered all the things I wanted her to know. I could've stayed there all day, having a sweet, private, last conversation with my girl.

Jack was standing nearby, talking to someone I couldn't see. His hand was on my waist, but his attention was on his companion. Then

I felt him move his hand away, and Ella Rae appeared. She put her head down on the casket too and draped an arm around my shoulder. "Hey," she said.

"Hey," I answered.

"What are you doing?"

"Just talking to Laine."

We stared at each other for a moment.

"I thought you were crying," she said.

"Why?"

"Because you're laid out over this coffin, dumb-ass."

"I was just talking to her, and the wood felt good against my face!"

"It's the bunch of people that think you are crying," she said. "I thought you were crying, now I bet they think we're *both* crying."

It never occurred to me that people would wonder what I was doing.

"This wood does feel good." Ella Rae began stroking the top of the coffin with her free hand. "It's very cool to the touch."

I made a face. "It's very cool to the touch? I have never heard you say anything like that in your life."

"What's wrong with that?" she asked.

"There's nothing wrong with it. You just don't speak like that. Laine speaks like that."

Ella Rae rolled her eyes. "Whatever. Anyway, people thought you were wailing. You know, it was very sad. They were even pointing at you."

"What? I'm not even upset!"

"About anything?"

"Well, other than Laine being dead and all!" I said, exasperated.

"I think we should get up now."

We started to move, but Ella Rae stopped me. "Wait!"

"What is it now?"

"Do you think we should cry? I mean, shouldn't we be upset? We can't just act like we were taking a nap."

"I can't cry right now. I'm not upset," I said.

"Then let's just stay like this until the funeral is over.".

"Perfect." I chuckled a bit. "We can ride the coffin out of here like a mechanical bull."

"Yes!" Ella Rae said. "And the band can play something out of *Urban Cowboy*."

That made me laugh. "It's a choir not a band, barhopper," I said. "This building is called a church."

"Oh yeah." She laughed too. "I knew I made the wrong turn."

Call it ridiculous, call it childish or irreverent, call it whatever you will, but we began to laugh. *Really* laugh. Looking back, I'm sure it was from anxiety, nerves, or any other condition that brings on a mild form of hysteria. But there was no stopping once it started.

"Creepy Guy would try to move us," I said as the giggles finally took over completely.

"Oh, I am sure," Ella agreed. "He would appear out of nowhere and just like a vampire, swoop down, catch us both around the neck, and then say, 'Hey, baby. How 'bout a little formaldehyde on the rocks at my place?'"

"Stop!" I said, my entire body shaking with laughter.

Ella Rae tried to tell me something else about the funeral director but was laughing too hard to get it out.

"Ladies," Jack said, suddenly standing behind us with an arm around us both. "I don't know what's going on, but most everyone in this church has become distraught watching the two of you. Now ... I know you're laughing—"

"What gave us away, Jack?" Ella Rae cackled. "It was her, wasn't it? She's so uncool in these situations."

"These situations?" I asked. "When's the last time you laid on a casket, Rae?"

"I was in Caskets are Us just yesterday, smarty-pants," she said. "I'm their new spokesperson. I laid on every casket in the house. I personally like the newer models because—"

"Okay, okay," Jack said. "Here's what we're about to do. I'm going to stand up with my arms around both of you, and you two are going to put your heads as deep into my chest as you can get them, and then we'll walk out the back. Got it?"

"Did you wear deodorant?" Ella Rae asked.

I nearly had to slap Laine's mahogany box that was so funny.

"What the hell is wrong with y'all?" he asked. "Now behave and hold on."

We walked out the back with our heads buried in Jack's suit jacket until he pushed us into the ladies room. Thankfully, no one else was in it because he came in too.

"What was that?" he demanded when we were safely behind the locked door.

Ella Rae sat down on the toilet and laughed so hard that she had to hold onto the wall. I sat on the floor and held my sides, shaking all over.

"The only sane one in the bunch is gone," Jack said and shook his head.

That was the funniest line of the day. We were nearly screaming with laughter now.

"Dead puppies, dead puppies, dead puppies," Ella Rae began to chant. That had been Laine's favorite mantra when she'd contracted the inappropriate giggles.

"And I don't want to know what that means," Jack said. "For God's sake, try to get it together in the next five minutes." He closed the door behind him.

After the laughter finally subsided, Ella Rae looked at me and smiled. "I can't tell you how much I needed that."

I nodded. "I know. Me too."

"This funeral is gonna suck, Carrigan," she said, somber now. "I wish we could skip over it, but then again, I want it to last for three days."

"Me too," I said again.

"I wish we could go back and do every bit of it again."

"Even the shitty parts. And even if I knew it would end all over again, just like this."

"We didn't let her leave here without ... without—"

"We left nothing unspoken," I assured her. "We turned over every stone, we shook every tree. We said it all."

Ella Rae shook her head. "I just can't remember saying it all. I would think of things I wanted to tell her when I was in bed at night, and then I couldn't remember what they were the next day."

"We told her everything," I said. "I promise we did."

She stood up and smoothed her dress. "Let's go. I'm ready now."

I took the hand she extended and got up off the floor. "I'm ready too."

Mrs. Jeanette had asked Ella Rae and me to sit in the front pew with the family, but we said that we would sit in the row behind. But she insisted we sit up front, saying, "You girls were her sisters. Where else would you be?"

Jack, Mitch, and Tommy were seated in the pew behind us, and I was thankful for that. Jack leaned up right before the service began and gave me a hug. "You'll do her proud, Carri. You always have." I was glad for that boost and hoped he was right. I had finally come up with what I wanted to say in the eulogy and then after last night had completely changed my mind. I hoped I could convey what was in my heart.

As soon as the music began, Ella Rae began to cry. I tried to think about something else, *anything* else. I didn't want to start the waterworks before I had to speak. I thought about Elle. I thought about football. I even thought about frog hunting. But nothing worked. I dabbed at my tears with a dainty hankie that had belonged to Laine.

"Friends, family, and loved ones, we are here to celebrate the life of Laine Elizabeth Landry," Reverend Martin began the service. "Let us open with a word of prayer."

I stared at my shoes while Reverend Martin prayed. I looked at their heels, the way they were made, the way the straps looked, the point of the toes. I did everything I could to avoid listening, short of putting my fingers in my ears. I finally heard him say, "Amen," and I looked up again. It was going to be a long hour or so.

"Laine came to see me last year, a few weeks after she'd been released from the hospital. She wanted to write the opening remarks for her funeral and asked me if I could help her with that. While this may seem a bit unorthodox to some, I intend to follow her wishes."

I looked at Ella Rae, and she shrugged slightly. Laine continued to surprise us.

"My name was Laine Elizabeth Landry. I was a daughter and a friend and a teacher and an aunt. Those were the most important things in my life and the things I hope to be remembered for. I am survived by the most wonderful mother a girl could ask for, Jeanette Landry, who gave me a treasured childhood and wings to fly when it was over. I love you, Mama. I had one brother, Michael, whose strength I always relied on and envied. I love you, Mike. Take care of my nieces. I had two sisters, Carrigan Whitfield and Ella Rae Weeks, who were indeed my sisters in every sense of the word. They showed me what unconditional love was time and time again. I am also survived by four nieces and a niece by proxy. It's a beautiful world, girls, but it's a tough world too. Ask for help when you need to, be good to your parents, and find true friends who will love you through it all. Remember, it isn't always blood that makes a family. I asked Michelle Lange to sing this song for all of you, my family. I loved you all very much. Thank you for everything. And don't worry ... I will save you all a seat."

Ella Rae was openly sobbing by now, as was Mrs. Jeanette, Michael, and almost everyone in the church. I was hanging on by a thread, but I was still okay. I was pretty sure I would make it without dissolving into a pool of tears. But then the music started, and my tears started with it. I recognized the chords immediately, and so did Ella Rae. She buried her face in my shoulder, and I put my arm around her as Michelle's sweet soprano began crooning a song we'd loved since junior high. It had been a number-one hit for a popular artist—a moving ballad about life, love, and loss, and it fit the occasion perfectly. I smiled through my tears, realizing that Laine had known all along what music would be played today and what would be said today. She only pretended to make us plan her funeral so we'd get used to the idea of having one and to stop being so frightened by the word. All this time, I thought I was the sly one of our trio, but it turned out to be Laine. She'd punked us. I wanted to laugh, but my tears were falling too fast, so I put my head against Ella Rae's and cried instead.

Mercifully, the music finally ended, and Reverend Martin stepped back to the podium. He began speaking of heaven and how Laine was there, healthy and whole again, visiting with her daddy and other loved ones who had gone before her. He spoke of green valleys and golden streets, of mansions and angels. I heard bits and pieces, ignoring what I could and feeling much like I did in Dr. Rougeau's office the day this nightmare first began. A dull roaring in my ears protected me from hearing it all. I didn't want to hear anything about heaven, especially the part where Laine was there now. I knew it was meant to comfort us, but it was no comfort to me. Laine was gone, and God took her. I was going to need a signed letter from Him to explain this.

The sound of my name jerked me back into the present. Reverend Martin had just announced that I would deliver the eulogy. I squeezed Ella Rae's hand and walked to the podium on automatic pilot. I still had no idea what would come out of my mouth.

I looked around at the packed church and sighed. Then from somewhere inside, I found my voice. "When Laine asked me to do this, my first reaction was to tell her no, I can't, and I won't. But in only the way she could, she wore me down. I just knew there was no possible way for me to tell you who Laine Landry was. I knew I could never make anyone understand what we had *all* lost. Then, in the last two days ... no, really, in the last few months ... I realized I didn't have to tell you who she was and what we lost because you all told us. It was obvious in the visits to the farm by her students, past and present. It was obvious by the flowers that arrived continuously, it was obvious in the phone calls and the cards and the food and the words you shared with us, especially in the last few days. You, the people of Bon Dieu Falls, told us things about Laine that we never knew. The lives she touched weren't exclusive to Ella Rae and me, although we probably thought they were."

I looked at Ella Rae, my sweet friend, still crying but smiling now too. "We lived in our bubble ... and we really, really loved our bubble." I smiled. "But Laine lived in the world. We only thought we were worldly and full of answers. Turns out we were just full of sh—" I glanced at Reverend Martin as the crowd rippled with laughter. "Well, we weren't quite what we thought we were. But she was," I said and looked down at the casket. "Laine was every bit what she seemed to be and then some. And you have validated that for us. So what I really need to say today is thank you. Thank you for loving her like we did and knowing her in some ways better than we did." I felt my control slipping and bit my lip hard for a moment. "All I could really tell you that you don't already know ... is how we bandaged each other's skinned knees and broken hearts and wounded pride ... and, selfish as it is, those are our stories. Laine's and Ella Rae's and mine. And I don't want to share them. Not yet, anyway. Thank you for loving our friend ... and for seeing in her all that we saw and more."

I stepped down from the podium, kissed Laine's coffin for the last time, and managed to make it back to Ella Rae's arms before the dam broke.

❦ *Chapter 20* ❦

I gathered the shawl closer around Elle's shoulders and pointed to her daddy turning into the driveway. "Who's that?" I asked her.

She began flailing her little arms and legs, her normal reaction whenever she saw him. She was only seven months old, but she was very bright, even if I do say so myself.

Jack was wearing a huge grin as he stepped out of the truck, which was his normal reaction when he saw Elle. I was surprised he didn't flail his arms and legs as well. He took the steps two at a time, planted a quick kiss on my lips, and scooped Elle out of my arms. She immediately began patting his face with her hands. "What did my two favorite girls do today while saddy was at work?" he asked her.

Elle responded by placing both her hands in his mouth and squealing.

I shook my head and smiled. Elle was becoming a poster child for a daddy's girl.

We'd been back in our own house for months since the week after Laine had died. I hated to leave the farm; we all did. But we needed to be back in our own places and back in the real world. Our protective bubble was no more. Laine's passing had forced us all to step back into reality and leave our magical realm where each moment was full of laughter and love. Those days had at times contradicted the impending doom that lay ahead. Even though we had all clung to the desperate hope for a miracle that never came, those days remain some of the most treasured times of my life. They had also changed me—no, not change. Change is not a large enough word. Those days had transformed me, I guess you could say. Every moment of every day was no longer about me and my wants and needs. I had never realized how selfish I was until the year Laine was dying. Oh, I would have done anything for Laine or Ella Rae even before then. But I had always examined every angle of a situation to assess what I could get out of it. What was in it for me? But my thinking had certainly changed over the past year. For the first time in my adult life, I felt like a grown-up.

Watching Jack and Elle, I felt the familiar tug on my heart. I loved them both so much and wondered for the millionth time how I could have ever entertained the idea of wanting something else or anybody else. Laine had told me time after time after time how much I loved Jack, but I was too stupid or full of pride to see it. But she'd always seen it. I sighed. Laine …

"You coming inside, Mommy?" Jack asked. "It's getting cool out here."

"I will in a few minutes, okay?" I said and smiled.

"Sure, baby," he said and kissed me again. "Take your time." He took Elle inside and left me in the porch swing.

Sweet Jack. He'd been so good to me since Laine died. He was unbelievably patient too. He always listened when I had ranted and raved about God and His logic. He was always attentive and understanding when I got in my occasional blue moods, like the one I was consumed by today. It wasn't depression; it wasn't even sadness. It was more like a quest for an answer. Why did Laine die? What possible good could come from it? Would I ever make peace with it? I needed resolution. I needed it to make sense.

I gazed across the street at her house and pictured her in the yard, spraying a speck of dirt off her back, watering flowers, and waving to me. I still had a hard time imagining anyone there but her. Mrs. Jeanette had mentioned putting Laine's house on the market a few weeks ago, and I became so frantic that Jack bought it. He walked in one evening after work, gave me a kiss, and handed me the deed. The relief was tremendous, and I had thanked him constantly for days. I still had no idea what we'd do with it, but for now, just owning it was enough. Ella Rae and I sometimes walked over and sat in the long-since-cleaned-out living room. I didn't know if that was a good or a bad thing, but it was certainly an emotional thing. I don't think a day passed since Laine died that Ella Rae didn't sob at least once. I didn't cry; I fretted and paced, and the questions hounded me, but I didn't cry. In fact, I hadn't cried since the day of the funeral.

I sighed and laid my head on the pillow of the porch swing. It wasn't a crippling time for me at least. I still went about my life, I loved my baby and my husband, and I put one foot in front of the other. I did what I was supposed to do. Yet the more people still offered condolences, the more perturbed I became. Especially the ones who said, "Some things just can't be explained," or "God's timing is perfect." What the hell did that even mean? I knew they were trying to make me feel better, but I wanted to bitch slap them all. Why say anything at all if you're only going to frustrate me more? Of course, that was wrong too. They were just trying to help.

I supposed this just what happened when you were grieving. The mood swings, I mean. Some days, every memory was funny and heartwarming and comforting. Other days, like today, I was mad and frustrated and confused, and the memories I clung to were unclear and unfocused. I was horrified that they would fade altogether. Laine's absence covered my world like a blanket. I hated these days. They usually began with my telling God about all the people in the world who didn't deserve to take another breath. Pedophiles, serial killers, and people who were mean to animals still walked around, laughing and talking and living, yet He took Laine? It made no sense to me. Where was the logic in that? If I lived to be one hundred, I would never understand it, and God still wasn't talking.

I started to wonder if He was even there at all. I needed an explanation, something tangible to make her death reasonable. I needed somebody to say to me, "Laine died so global warming would subside," or "Laine died so there would be peace in the Middle East," or even "Laine died so teenagers would no longer suffer from acne." Something! Anything! I had to have some answers, but I had no idea where to start.

Church left me even more confused and sad. I couldn't sit there without thinking of that awful mahogany box that was now covered in dirt. I certainly couldn't linger on that thought for long.

Mama had sent Reverend Martin over a few times, even though she'd denied doing it, but he'd only made me feel guilty when he said I should never question God. I toyed with consulting a medium, but Ella Rae had nearly fainted from the thought. Such a Baptist. So I mostly just sat in this swing and pondered. Sometimes I looked up at the night sky and asked Laine if she was there. If she was in the paradise she had assured me she'd punched her ticket for. But like God, she didn't answer either.

Enough. I stood up and peered in the window to my living room. Jack and Elle were sitting on the floor, playing, and once again, I physically felt my love for both of them. The ever-present questions about Laine would still be here tomorrow. I went inside to join my family.

The next morning was cold and rainy. I loved snuggling in bed with Jack. Just like me, Elle would sleep for twelve straight hours, usually from eight p.m. to eight a.m. Everyone told me what a blessing that was and told horror stories about their children's sleeping habits. Charlotte Freeman said neither of her kids had ever slept through the night, and they were three and four years old. I couldn't imagine. Elle's nocturnal habits left an awful lot of time for her father and me to reconnect, and boy, did we reconnect. Jack was trying his best to reconnect that morning, but I slapped his hand when he slipped it under the covers.

"No," I said laughing. "Elle will be awake in five minutes!"

"All I need is three," he said, nuzzling my neck.

"Then *hell* no!" I laughed again and scooted away from him. As if on cue, Elle began moving in her bed beside us. "See?"

"I'm gonna have to have a talk with this girl," Jack said and leaned over me to pick her up.

"About guys like you," I said. "Ugh ... you're squashing me."

"Good morning, little one," he said to Elle as she rubbed her sleepy eyes.

She smiled, squealed, and flailed her legs.

Jack got up, changed her diaper, and then got back into bed, depositing Elle between us. She laughed and cooed and smiled and then demanded her breakfast. She was such a happy baby. I loved mornings like this. My blue moods never made an appearance during those moments.

"Are you going to work?" I asked, hoping he'd say no.

"Na," he answered, making me smile. "Not much going on, and it's cold and rainy. I'd rather spend today here."

"Yay!" I said to Elle. "Daddy's hanging with us today!"

Jack began rubbing my thigh. "How much longer until she takes a nap?" he asked, winking at me.

"You are awful!" I accused, but his hand sure felt good. I bit my lip. "After lunch," I said and smiled.

A knock on the front door interrupted our fun.

"I'll go," Jack said and pulled on a t-shirt.

Elle had finished nursing, and I was buttoning my shirt when Jack came back into the bedroom with a huge box in his arms and a strange expression on his face.

"What's that?" I asked.

"I don't know," he said. "It's addressed to you and Ella Rae … from Laine."

I stared at him. "What do you mean?"

He put the box on the chaise and gestured toward it. "See for yourself."

I picked up Elle and walked over to look at the large cardboard box. Jack was right. It was addressed to Ella Rae and me at my street address in Laine's impeccable handwriting; I would recognize it anywhere. The return address read, "Laine E. Landry, Heaven." I continued to stare at it, but I didn't touch it or move. "What *is* this?"

Jack put his arm around me. "I don't know, sweetheart," he answered. "The UPS man brought it, not the archangel Michael. Are you alright?"

I didn't answer, just continued looking at the box. Of course I knew the archangel Michael didn't bring it, just as I knew it hadn't come from heaven as the return address suggested. But where had it come from? And where had it been? Who sent it? What was in it?

Jack took Elle from me. "Listen," he said. "Elle's already had breakfast, we have three or four hours of cushion. I'll get her dressed and take her out to the farm with me. Why don't you call Ella Rae and open the box together?"

I sat down on the chaise beside the box. "Okay," I said absently and studied the handwriting again. I reached for the phone and called Ella Rae. She promised to arrive in ten minutes.

Jack and Elle hadn't been gone long when Ella Rae busted through the front door. "Where is it?" she asked.

I pointed to the box. "There."

She folded her arms and stood beside it, inspecting it without touching. "What's in it?

"I don't know, Ella Rae. I obviously haven't opened it."

"You have no clue what's inside it?" she asked, but it sounded more like an accusation.

"Do you think I shit an X-ray machine?"

"You are such a smart-ass," she said, rolling her eyes.

"And you're such a dumb-ass. You see the box is still taped shut."

She poked at the box with a pen from Jack's desk.

I stared at her, wondering once again what it was like to live in her world. "Laine ain't in the box, Rae."

"Yes, I know," she said, looking at me like I was crazy, and then added, "Open it."

"*You* open it."

"It's addressed to you," she said indignantly.

"It's addressed to *both* of us," I corrected her.

"But it's got your street number on it. She must've wanted you to open it. If she'd wanted me to open it, it would've had my street number on it, but the UPS man doesn't come to my part of town until after lunch. Especially on rainy days ... but sometimes he comes around noon if—"

"Oh crap, Ella Rae," I said, as our conversation took a familiar turn toward the ridiculous. "Go get me a knife."

She ran out of the bedroom and was back a few seconds later with the largest knife from my kitchen.

I took it from her. "We aren't skinning a hog, Rae," I said, examining the blade.

"It was the first one I saw."

We stood in front of the box and looked at each other for a moment.

"This is so stupid," I said finally. "I don't know what we think is in there." I began cutting the tape from the top as Ella Rae peered over to get the first look. When I pulled the top apart, at least six or seven spring snakes flew out in every direction. Ella Rae and I screamed in unison, jumping up and down in place like cartoon characters.

I picked up one of the snakes and flung it across the room in a fit of hysterical laughter. "Almost gave me a heart attack!" I said, my hand on my chest.

"Why did she do that?" Ella Rae shouted from her seat on the floor where she'd fallen. "If she wasn't dead, I'd kill her!"

I looked at the big white poster board inside the box. Laine had written, "Gotcha! LOL! LOL! LOL!" in big purple letters with smiley faces all over.

I read the message out loud and handed Ella Rae the poster board.

"Ugh!" she said, finally standing up. "Ha ha! Very funny, Laine!"

I wiped away the laughter tears and looked back in the box. There was a huge leather-bound book that appeared to be some sort of journal. I took it out of the box and laid it on the bed. Two more just like it were underneath. I opened the first one and read the inscription aloud. "For Carrigan, with your fiery spirit and huge personality. You took me places I could have never gone. When you ask 'why,' and I KNOW you will, pick up this gift. I love you always, and I'll see you again. Laine."

I looked at Ella Rae, who was, of course, crying, and handed her the next journal. She opened it, wiped her eyes, and read that inscription aloud too. "For Ella Rae, with your childlike innocence and mean right hook. You showed me what it was like to love someone so much that you'd fight for them. Literally. When you cry, and I KNOW you will, pick up this gift. I love you, and I'll see you again. Laine."

We both began flipping through the pages filled with pictures from grammar school until our time at the farm just months ago. Laine had filled both books with ticket stubs, napkins, notes, matchbooks, a receipt from a bar when the tab between Ella Rae and me was two hundred dollars, a program from a school play, and a piece of the uniforms we'd worn when we'd won the state softball championship. Pieces of our lives were scattered across every page, and Laine had written something under every memento. Ella Rae and I sat on the bed, comparing our books, reliving moments, laughing, and remembering. I was amazed. The books were huge and full.

"This is what she did in her room all the time," I said.

"You're right!" Ella Rae agreed. "I'm sure it is!"

We both sat in silence on my bed and continued looking at our books, comparing things, laughing at things, and marveling at the amount of time Laine had obviously spent putting these together. We tried to guess where the box had come from, who had sent it, and where had it been.

We must've sat there an hour and a half, just remembering. Everything Laine had included in the books had a story with it. When I finally reached the last page, there was Laine's perfect penmanship again, but this time as a letter, or a long note, I guess you'd say. This I read in silence.

An American writer, Rita Mae Brown, wrote, 'I still miss those I loved who are no longer with me, but I find I am grateful for having loved them. The gratitude has finally conquered the loss.' I know you are struggling with my death. But it's been six months, and that's long enough to bang your head against the wall—PLEASE don't even try to deny that, I've seen you do it a thousand times when you can't rationalize something. You go round and round and round until it makes you nuts. STOP! To use a phrase you have always despised, it is what it is. I want you to remember me, but I don't want you to get lost in remembering. Feed a stray dog when you get lonesome for me. Check on some of the older ladies in town that have no help when you get lonesome for me. Or better yet, go to church! I bet you haven't been twice since the funeral. I'm not in the casket, Carrigan, and I'm not at the cemetery ... I never was. Now go live, and stop obsessing on this! I'm so proud of you, of the mother you are and the wife you have become. (And oh, about Jack ... I hate to say I told you so, but ... I

TOLD YOU SO!) By the way, how'd you like the song at the funeral? Okay, that was a cheap shot, but it was our song, so I had to. Take care of your family, take care of Rae and Tommy, and take care of yourself. I love you. Always. Laine.

I swept my fingers across the written words. I opened my mouth to read them to Ella Rae and then stopped. I wouldn't share them yet. I knew I would one day, but not today. Today I wanted to keep them to myself and read them over and over and over. Besides, Ella Rae was reading her own note, smiling ... and crying.

I realized suddenly, in a moment that stunned me, that the journal in my lap had done more than give me mementos of my adored Laine and our cherished time together. I felt different now than I had in all the months since her death. I felt ... untroubled, maybe for the first time in *years*. Had God just answered a thousand questions? I was unexpectedly filled with gratitude for having known Laine. I was most fortunate to have had her in my life—not everyone had a Laine. And I was grateful for so much more. I looked around me, at my home, the pictures of my family, Jack, and my baby. I looked at Ella Rae sitting beside me, quietly thumbing through her own journal. To say that God had blessed me would forever be an understatement.

Laine had been Ella Rae's and my voice of reason. She'd been our calm during a storm. She'd been our conscience and constant companion ... and now, she'd become our comforter. Memories that had been foggy in my mind were suddenly as real as the journal I was holding, and they flooded my soul like the tears that were *finally* flowing from my eyes. It was the sweetest release I had ever felt. I grabbed Ella Rae's sandpaper hand and kissed it. I could *hear* Laine's laughter, I could *see* her face, I could *feel* her around us. I realized that day, sitting on my bed with Ella Rae, that even though Laine wasn't across the street or physically sitting there with us, her spirit surrounded us and always would. Laine lived on every day, she was just somewhere else—and the peace and acceptance that had eluded me for months was delivered to me in a box from heaven.

Epilogue

*F*ive years later, life has gone on. In many ways, things have remained the same; such is life in a small town. But that isn't a bad thing. It's comforting knowing that Otis will be on the street corner by the post office when I go into town, nursing his ever-present forty-ounce beer, that I have to steer Elle away from Miss Lucy at the ballpark for fear she'll swat at her, and even that Bethany Wilkes will be dressed impeccably at any function I see her... even if her clothes are several sizes larger now. I'm guessing that bakery thing worked out after all.

Ella Rae and I have found a wonderful way to share Laine's enthusiasm for helping other people. We started the Laine Landry Foundation that assists older residents of Bon Dieu Falls with things like transportation, groceries, and medicine. Several of Laine's former students volunteer and provide much-needed help like mowing lawns for the elderly, planting flowers in their yards, tending their gardens, and shopping for them. The foundation is privately funded, and we have transformed the annual crawfish boil into our big fund-raiser for the year. The support has been overwhelming.

Laine's house has become our office and also a place for older folks to gather. Miss Jeannette cooks for them several times a week while they play cards, watch movies, or just visit. Mamie even comes by some mornings to leave her famous cinnamon rolls. The older folks are a complete joy to be around, and Elle thinks she has a dozen sets of grandparents, white and black alike, because they all dote on her. They teach her all sorts of things from the proper way to shoot marbles to the fine art of cursing. She picked up a coffee cup at home a week ago and threw it back down declaring, "That son of a bitch is hot." Thank you, Mr. Henry. I thought Jack would pop trying to hide his laughter. I explained to her gently that wasn't language we used. She said, "But you called MeMe's horse a son of a bitch when he kicked you." I have a ways to go with this little redhead.

Mitch is doing well too. He hasn't remarried but seems to be happier nowadays. He left Dallas and moved to Natchitoches, which is closer to home. He owns a financial advisory firm and takes care of the money for the foundation. He's a whiz at his job and has really helped us grow. Of course, his heart is in the project as well. I have met his son a few times, who seems like a great young man and has his father's curly hair and good looks. Ella Rae and I have both tried introducing Mitch to some friends of ours, but he keeps saying, "Not yet." Perhaps Laine was right. If you love someone right the first time, once is enough.

Ella Rae and Tommy had a little boy last year, Thomas James Weeks Jr., or TJ, as we call him. He is adorable and looks just like his mother with blond hair and brown eyes. Ella Rae never missed a beat when she was pregnant, jogging with me every day until she was about eight months along. I finally made her quit. I wasn't interested in delivering him on the side of the road. Ella Rae is my co-chairman at the foundation, so we are thankfully still together every day. She single-handedly oversees the Laine Landry Memorial Softball Tournament every year that continues to grow and prosper and provides scholarships to two graduating seniors every year. Last year, we were able to give each recipient five thousand dollars, and this year we are on track to give even more.

Jack and I are stronger than ever. It's hard to believe we just celebrated our fifteenth anniversary. He took me to the farm … for a picnic. The days behind us are just that, behind us. I sometimes feel sorry for couples who have never gone through anything, who have never had their limits tested. There's no doubt in my mind that Jack and I can weather any storm life throws our way. We'll be adding another member to our family soon, another girl. Jack says we're stopping after this one; I think he fears he'll drown in the hormones around here after awhile. Elle is very excited about a little sister. She is totally convinced that TJ is her little brother, and that there is no need for her father and me to give her one. She wants to name the baby Bubbles and is very adamant about it, and while we have yet to decide on a proper name, I fear Bubbles may stick. Thank God she's into bubbles these days. If it were a year ago, we may have had to call the baby Sponge Bob.

Oh, and the third journal in the box from heaven? It was for Elle. A handwritten guide for every year from Elle's first through her twenty-first birthday, things Laine wanted her to know, to see, to do. Every year on her birthday, Elle gets a card from Laine and a charm for the bracelet she got on her first birthday. I still have no idea where they come from, who sends them, or how they remember. But Elle gets ridiculously excited when she receives them and talks about her "Laine book" all the time. It's her favorite bedtime story. Sometimes she asks me, "Mommy, can Laine see us? Is she watching us?" I tell her, without any doubt in my mind, "Yes, sweetheart. She watches us all."

CPSIA information can be obtained at www.ICGtesting.com
Printed in the USA
LVOW11s1409120614

389798LV00001B/131/P

9 781483 400877